Rhydian's
Quest

Rhydian's Quest

V S Jones

Book Guild Publishing
Sussex, England

First published in Great Britain in 2011 by
The Book Guild Ltd
Pavilion View
19 New Road Brighton,
BN1 1UF

Typeset in Baskerville by Ellipsis Books Limited, Glasgow

Printed in Great Britain by CPI Antony Rowe

A catalogue record for this book is available from The British Library.

ISBN 978 1 84624 547 3

To Jean [Redkite] 1949–2010
Who sowed the first seed for my story,
and my other cyberspace friends for the help
and encouragement they gave to me throughout
the writing of my 'saga'.

A donation from the sale of each copy of *Rhydian's Quest* will be made to Crossroads Care Wales.

Having worked with carers for nearly 20 years I am delighted to support this imaginative and thought-provoking book. Many families with caring responsibilities have an unexpected road to travel, with many twists and turns. I am thrilled that Crossroads Care will benefit from sales of this book, which will allow us to offer support to carers as they journey through life.

Angela Roberts, Director, Crossroads Care Wales.

www.crossroads.org.uk

Part One
The Journey

The Squire

The young squire, soon to be knighted,
Sat cleaning the saddle for his beloved
Horse. Tomorrow a bright new caparison
Would cover the fine leather, crimson
And yellow, colours to banish sadness
From anyone's heart. Tomorrow was
To be a joyous day, when he left behind
Childhood, and became a man. His mind
Wandered to four years ago, to the parting
Gift his father gave to him when leaving
Home, to train as a page in the household
Of an unknown knight. A child yet, not bold,
But saddened in spirit on that cold morn
In the stable, where lay a colt, newly born.
'He is yours, in a short year you will return
Home, then you both will have much to learn.
Train him well for he will become a friend
To trust in, on whom your life may depend.
We must leave him now, in his mothers care.'
Returning home a squire, who must prepare,
Grow into manhood. The young colt he trained,
Cadair Idris, after the mountain named.
On the morrow he would become a knight,
A long vigil awaited him through the coming night,
To choose his path, to follow where it will take
Him, clear his mind, prepare for vows to make

The Night Before

The day begins to close, the vigil draws nigh,
Rhydian made Cadair's bed, straw piled high,
Tending to him in his final hours as a child.
Taking pleasure in the menial task, he filled
The rick, then rested, with his head buried
As oft before, in the warmth of Cadair's side.
He leant against the flank of his horse, aware
That tonight his soul would lay strangely bare.
His mother had ready a plain silken shift, white,
The symbol of purity, waiting in nervous delight
To wash and robe him, to give him water to drink.
For today he had fasted, releasing his mind to think.
As the sun set on the day, it cast a rich, fiery, glow,
Dark shadows crept across the castle keep, a slow
Dark veil falling as he entered the Chapel. Here alone,
In this quiet sanctuary, like so many before to atone
For man's sins, in contemplation of what will follow
To become a knight, and so to take his sacred vow.

The Knighting

In the small castell chapel the soft rays of the morning
Sun slipped through a window, finding a youth, placing
Round his head a halo. So still, like a carved angel,
Kneeling before the altar. Distant sounds broke the spell
Many voices, chanting hymns. Slowly the youth stirred
Stretching his cramped limbs, listening, surely he heard
His name carried on the breeze as the throng drew near.
He felt calm, a sense of ease drove away an unnatural fear.
He stepped out to await them. Many visitors from far around
Gathered, now was the time for old friends to be found,
For new ones made. Suddenly a ripple of expectation
Ran through the crowd, who would make the creation
Of the new knight? Rumour abounded, a definite sighting
Had been made of royal garb, could it be a princeling?
Striding firmly to the green, still in a trance-like bliss,
Came Rhydian, to all the speculation, oblivious.
Then, stopping, as he reached the appointed place
He caught the eye of his father, his mothers face
In view, he wondered why none came to greet him
But held back as if in awe. Then out of shadows dim
Came a tall figure and he saw the royal dragon of Wales
Blazoned across the shield. A symbol of knightly tales.
Raised high, ready to wield, was a mighty sword
Held firm in the hand of Llewellyn whose very word
Was law throughout the land. His voice rang out strong
'Approach me without fright, your time is now, you belong
With the chosen few, the right to bear arms and so defend
Your home, protect the weak, give sustenance and befriend
The poor, remaining meek in thought, with spirit free,
Son of Powys, bow before your liege.' On bended knee
He entered the tales of lore, to follow the rules of chivalry.

The sword, with a flash of light rested on his shoulder,
 gently,
'Arise Sir Rhydian – I lay claim to you, for you are my
 knight
I command you to follow your conscience and God's light.'

The Evening After

As calm descended, in the quiet aftermath of the day
Where all the guests having left, now making their way
Home, some to castles, some to cottages, holding fast
To their memories, for they had seen their prince at last,
The new knight meditated. Many thoughts filled his mind,
Ideas chased around in circles, no answers could he find.
'What ails you, Sir Rhydian? Tonight you have the right
To any lady of your choice. Go have your fill of true
    delight.'
Prince Llewellyn laughed at the look of pain upon his face.
'Last night, on my vigil, I made a vow, in that sacred place,
To be a true knight, to honour the code, protect the weak
Serve my Liege and our Lord. Carnal pleasures not to seek
Until true love I find.' The Prince looked on this comely
Youth, there a reflection of himself when young could see.
'I wish you to join my household, up North, at Castell y
    Bere
I want you to travel alone, take the high roads, with the
    deer
And wolves for company.' He held him there just by the eye
Turning, he walked away. His word was law and with a sigh
Sir Rhydian knew that he must follow. Slowly, in his heart
Grew a glow of anticipation, for he would play the part
Of Sir Peredur. A journey, mayhap a quest, beckoned,
In which to prove himself worthy to call a prince his friend.

The Journey Begins

As the time for his journey drew nigh
Sir Rhydian polished his sword well,
His shield now bearing his own arms.
A bright blazon, so all could tell
What manner of man this knight was.
The colour of Or for generosity
Of spirit with ordinaries of rich
Gules for strength and magnanimity.
His courage, strength and virtue
Shown by unicorns, a springing
Stag bearing witness to peace
And harmony. A Harp to bring
Mystical heaven closer to earth.
Under his surcoat was no armour
This quest was not one of battle
But a seeking of inner succour.
To find his true path to travel
Would be his challenge, comforts
Of home left far behind, taking
Counsel from his own thoughts.
His father called him to his side
'Before you go, your way to wend
Come with me to choose your
Guard, companion and friend.'
Together they went into the stable,
Where the castle great hounds lay.
'You will need protection from
The wolves that hide during the day
Then hunt at night. Take the strongest,
Bravest of the pack, one who kills
Swiftly and silently. Who can follow
A cold trail across the rugged hills

This will keep you safe and fed.'
Heeding these words, he took measure
Of every one, seeking a connection,
Taking his time, deciding at leisure.
One bitch, the smallest there, returned
His gaze. Gently he called to her
Quietly she rose, standing by his side
He rested his hand on her soft fur.
'This is my dog, in whom I trust.
Her name will be Cyfaill.'
His father was rather troubled
'I hope you have chosen well
This dog is not the strongest
Of the pack.' 'I am satisfied
Her heart is brave, though 'tis true
That, like me, she is yet untried.'
Then as the sun rose up in the sky
Sir Rhydian mounted his steed,
Hound behind, riding out of Castell Du
To begin his quest, his noble deed.

Down To Earth

From the distant castle tower
His mother, watching him depart
Sending prayers upon the wind
Felt a deep sorrow in her heart.
Her son, her child, all alone
To make an arduous journey
To follow the wild forbidding
Mountain path. 'Why leave me
Behind, to seek your fortune?
This fair castle is a forlorn place
Without laughter, without smiles,
Without the light that from your face
Shines, radiating from within
And lighting up the dark corners
When darkness falls. I cannot bear
The times to come, now who honours
Me with their presence, bringing me
Stories of deeds of daring from afar?
But most of all, who will protect you,
Keep you from crossing the final bar?'
For her gallant son in high excitement
No such worries disturbed the pleasure
Of riding on a fine day, the warm sun
On his back. To have time, the leisure
To think in peace, of unbroken silence
Except for the natural sounds so often
Drowned by loud voices, raised in anger.
The desire for quiet set him apart when
Training both as a page and squire.
Now he listened to the river flowing
Over rocks, doves cooing in the trees
Leaves swaying, with the wind blowing

Across the long grass beside the banks.
Cadair, eager to go, began to prance,
Jolting Rhydian back to the present,
With a rude awakening to his trance
Unseated him, landing on the ground.
Cyfaill, thinking this was a fine game
Ran around with glee, great paws
Splashing mud on hose, the same
On surcoat. Cadair, saddle slipping.
Reins entangled, stood close by.
With laughter welling up inside
He remounted, letting Cadair fly
Faster and faster they went
Along the river-banks, running for joy
No longer a solemn knight just
A horse, a hound and a boy.

The Maid

Their wild headlong charge
Slowed down to a gentle pace.
The sun was high in the sky
Before they found a resting place
Where Rhydian washed himself
In the river, revelling in the cold
Water, spread out his clothes
To dry. There in the grassy fold
He fell asleep, with Cyfaill
And Cadair, keeping watch.
He dreamt of Uther Pendragon,
Of Myrddyn and the witch
Morgain. Tales of yore taking
Him to the magic kingdom
At Caerleon where Arthur
Held court. Suddenly a random
Sound woke him, senses alert,
What caused his sleep to be upset?
The sound came again, close by,
Cadair and Cyfaill stayed quiet,
Unconcerned by any noise.
Then Rhydian noticed, by a stream
A young girl, all alone singing
Softly, still in the thralls of dream
He wondered if this was Nimue.
Walking towards her he sang too,
Their voices mingling in perfect
Harmony. He sank deep into
Her blue eyes, as she, turning,
Faced him. She gave a mighty cry
Of laughter, making Rhydian stop.
Then the truth dawned of why

The romantic time had passed.
With his face turning crimson
He fled in hurry to his friends,
To put his clothes back on.

A Dream

With modesty regained
He returned to find the maiden.
The stream where she had sat
Was empty. Heart heavy laden
He searched, the sound of her
Voice circling inside his mind
The smile in her bright blue eyes
Followed him, daring him to find
Her again. Sadly he called Cyfaill
And remounted Cadair, once more
Journeying westwards towards
An unknown future. He was sure
One day their paths would cross
Again, so with his spirits raised
He rode towards a deserted castle
Where wild herds now grazed.
Here he had played with boyhood
Friends and became in those games
The heroes of legend and myth
Whose exploits ensured the names
Lived on in poetry and song.
He wandered beneath the walls
Of earth where the grass grew.
From tribal memory came the calls
Of wounded men and frightened
Women, the sound of arrows
Whistling overhead and swords
Clashing, the caws of carrion crows
Waiting in anticipation of a feast.
A shiver came over him, a cold
Mist was descending in the valley,
Swirling and beginning to enfold

The three companions. The hills
Appeared to be floating in a sea
Of cloud. An old road led upwards,
Straight as the trunk of a rowan tree,
Taking the travellers away from old
Battle scenes to new places as yet
Undiscovered. Now, as Rhydian left
This valley behind, Cadair began to fret
Wanting to climb high, Cyfaill too felt
The desire to leave the mist behind.
As they followed the track upwards
The trees thinned, shelter hard to find.
At the summit the sun began to set
He cast around for a place to camp.
The hilltops were bare, odd shapes
Marked out in stone walls. With damp
Clinging to their clothes he found
No means of making a fire to keep
Them dry and safe from attackers.
Feeling lost and afraid, emotions deep
Within rose to the surface, he sank
To the ground, a warm head at rest
On his knee as Cyfaill lay beside him.
With Cadair close by, feeling blessed,
Sir Rhydian slept, a child protected.
Just before dawn he was roused
From his slumber, not yet awake
He stayed very still, as he watched,
Orderly rows of soldiers passed him by,
The rhythmic sound of marching feet
Seemed to shake the ground and echo
Inside his head, with a constant beat.
They were clad in strange uniforms,
The like of which he had never seen
Before. Behind came sweating horses

Pulling small carts, Rhydian being keen
To see more, crept closer, he looked
In surprise at the scene, high walls,
Buildings where there had been none
The night before. He could hear calls
Across the hills, in a strange yet familiar
Language. Cadair and Cyfaill had vanished.
He was all alone and fear gripped his
Being. He began to pray and wished
He could disappear. A soldier went by
So close he could almost touch him,
Yet he remained unseen, as if he was
Invisible. Rhydian crossed himself, a dim
Recollection of stories long since heard,
About soldiers from a distant land,
Sweeping through Cymru, devastating
The countryside with a heavy hand.
They left buildings and forts and roads
Such as the one from Tre'rcastell
To this place. He heard two men talking,
Some words he understood and could tell
There was great excitement and plots
Afoot. As dawn broke over the hillside
The troops melted away, the buildings,
Horses, all were no more, just the wide
Open spaces, with Cadair quietly grazing
And Cyfaill, twitching, still chasing coneys
In her sleep. He pondered, was it a dream?
Searching around by where the soldiers
Had stood he saw coins, in proud relief,
A face, with leaves encircling his head.
Trying to recall the words he had heard
Spoken, what had those soldiers said?
One word he knew – 'Aurum - aur!'

A Change Of Plan

Pondering on last night's events,
Rhydian made his way down the hillside,
Cadair picking his way down a path
So steep he began to slip and slide
Yet taking great care of his charge.
Gradually the going grew softer
The scrub began to give way to
Fields of lush grass with clear water
To drink from. Refreshing themselves
They made their way to the distant
River, looking for a place to cross.
Far to the west he saw an encampment
Of many men and horses moving below
Castle walls. Warily he moved northwards
Memories of tales told on dark nights
Around the fires of home, how the hordes
Of English soldiers fought the Lord Rhys
To recapture the castle built by a Norman
Knight. When he died his sons continued
To fight, who held the fort had command
Of the valley, where three rivers joined.
Rhydian forded the nearest of these,
Cadair had no need to swim, his height
Keeping the rider dry, striding with ease
Along the river bed, Cyfaill, in danger
Of being taken by the current swelled
With mountain rain, slim body shivering.
Rhydian leant down, holding fast, pulled
Her onto the pommel of his saddle.
Cadair arching his neck and with pride,
Carried his friends to the other bank.
There, looking for shelter in which to hide

17

Rhydian noticed the same stone shapes
As last night, stone walls laid out in square
Patterns. Rough tracks leading towards
The north west, in parts covered by spare
Grass but without a doubt a roadway.
In the way he had learnt when a squire
He gathered sticks, moss and dry bark
Placed them on a stone, ready to make a fire.
Taking a small silk net out of his pack
He called Cyfaill, hobbled Cadair and headed
For the river. In a quiet backwater he set
His trap, Cyfaill watched, then joyfully bounded
Through the water, silver drops splashing
Behind. Brown-backed fish, with the sunlight
Flashing along their sleek sides darted
Into the net, then with opening closed tight
Dinner was caught, they returned to Cadair.
His plan had been had to follow the river,
Now there was a need to avoid the castle.
Rhydian looked longingly at the track, a sliver
Of stone cutting a straight furrow, beckoning
Him to follow. He recalled last night,
Surely the soldiers would take this route?
Mind made up, knowing he was right,
He resumed his journey, on to the wild moor.

Maid Or Vision?

The flood plain between the two rivers
Offered no shelter, Rhydian rode fast across
Keeping far to the north of the castle
Resting on the bank, stones covered in moss
He looked out at the fast flowing current
Then touching his friend he spoke gently,
'Cadair Idris, you needs must be as strong
As your namesake to carry us safely
Through the water, I put my trust in you.'
Then, holding fast to Cyfaill he rode
Straight into the foaming water.
With steady purpose Cadair bore his load
Over the river. Suddenly he paused,
Nostrils flaring, head held high.
Cyfaill quivered, pressing close by.
Rhydian listened to the wind, a soft sigh
Seemed to be caressing them, pulling
His gaze downwards to the river bed
Where the bright stones shimmering,
Changed shape into blue eyes, framed
By long dark hair. The sound of music
Swirled inside his head, bewitching
Him with a voice of such rare purity,
That was not of mortals, but enticing
Him to sink deep beneath the waves.
Filling his young soul with the desire
To follow, to join in the eternal song.
Then the spell broke, leaving a fire,
Smouldering forever, in his heart.

Inspiration

Cadair reached the far side, leaping up the bank
Took off down the old track not stopping until
Llandyffri was far behind, Cyfaill running
As if the devil were chasing her out of hell.
The desperate race gradually slowing down
As their panic grew less, till hidden from sight,
They rested in a grassy hollow. Drawing deep
Breaths of air, shamed by his fearful flight,
Rhydian dismounted from his sweating horse.
With Cyfaill's body pressing against his side
He took handfuls of grass and with rhythmic
Strokes dried his destrier. Feeling pride
In the powerful muscles and glossy coat,
With each steady sweep he regained control
Of his own fears. A smile crept across his face
Fired by memories of eyes, deep as the pool
Where Tylwyth dwelt, framed by witches' hair
That curled upwards, colour as black as jet
Set in a timeless face, and though it belonged
In the realms of myth and legend, yet
Was still of this time and this place.
The friends needed to rest and eat
Here was lush grass and water with
Game a-plenty to hunt, a fresh leat
To drink from, a perfect place to stay.
The fire cast its shadows all around
As replete and at peace, music filled
His mind, the evocative sound
Of her voice entered into his soul
Where he took the notes, creating
A symphony of song which swelled

Inside him until he too was singing,
Softly at first, increasing in power,
Echoes rebounding off the hillsides
Chasing each other, notes repeating
In a never-ending canon that rides
Across the valley in joyful praise,
Finally, all passion spent, he slept
Like an innocent babe, unknowing
That those who heard his song had wept.

The Old Road

The morning sun slipped over the gorse
Casting a rosy hue over the sleeping boy
Lying curled around his hound, his horse
Quietly grazing, yet watchful of his charge.
As the rays touch his face he begins to stir
Stretching his lithe body he reaches out
To his friends, hand ruffling Cyfaill's fur
Calling to Cadair he prepares to continue
The journey. His eyes sweeping ahead
Seeking trace of the old track heading
Straight over the highland, a faint thread,
But for those who look, a certain sign
To follow. All day long they travelled,
At peace with the world. They drank
Water from streams, keeping well fed
With game hunted with skill and guile.
For one day more they rode the track
Until the path led down the hillside.
Here the land seemed strange, black
Scars cutting through shrubs, large flat
Areas, with steep sides, like a giant stair
Winding round in a spiral leading down
To a large pit surrounded by rock, bare
Where trees and plants struggled to gain
A foothold in this land. Casting around,
Rhydian sought a sheltered place to sleep
In the waste tips of this disturbed ground
Where haunted souls seemed to remain.
He had not rested for long when a low
Sound woke him, voices from above
Drifting on the air. Figures in the glow

Of a flaming torch moved toward him.
Closer they came, until he could hear
Them speak. The same strangely familiar
Language he had heard before, then, clear
And loud he heard the word he knew 'Aur.'
He watched the two climb upwards, past
Other figures sleeping until they reached
A rocky outcrop, then disappeared, so fast
He almost lost them. Far below the land
Had changed, no trees to be seen, just soil
Well dug, piled high onto earthy heaps.
Mist began to swirl around, a clammy coil
Entwining round Rhydian, as if an invisible
Hand reached across him, blocking the scene
From view. Unable to see he returned, back
To his camp to ponder on what it could mean.

In A Hole

In the morning he tethered Cadair
To a low tree, keeping Cyfaill right
Beside him he headed for the place
Where he lost the two men from sight.
As he reached the rocky wall, suddenly,
The ground under his feet gave way,
And he was falling, down into a cold
Dank hole, where no sunlight could play.
He reached the bottom, falling heavily,
And lay there, winded, Cyfaill howled
In fear, the sound echoing down to him.
Standing up, he stretched out and found
He was unable to reach the top. He felt
The wall of stone, smooth as glass, cold
And slippery, with centuries of moss
Growing where there was no handhold.
Missing nothing Rhydian ran his hands
Everywhere. There was one stone, much
Bigger than the rest, in texture it was
Different, feeling rougher to the touch.
He tried to move it, digging his fingers
Along its edge. Excitement increasing
As gradually he pulled the whole stone
Forward, taking his dagger, gouging
The sides until it came right away.
Putting his hand into the small cavity
He pulled out an old leather pouch.
Covered in slime, and feeling heavy.
Tucking it inside his jerkin, he tried
To climb out. With his dagger he made
Crevices in the wall, but to no avail.

None to help, his hopes began to fade.
He thought of home, of his parents
Waiting in vain for news of his travel.
He thought of his beloved Cadair,
Of Cyfaill, who had left him in peril
To rot in this forgotten oubliette.
Just when hope had died away
He heard sounds, getting closer,
Afraid to call out, he began to pray.
Cyfaill's loud bark rang out, then
Something wet touched his hand.
Rhydian caught hold of a silken rope,
As Cadair, answering his command
Pulled back and Rhydian scrambled out.
A joyous hound, looking very pleased
With herself, covered him in wet licks,
Flecked with blood. As Rhydian released
The rope, he saw it was Cadair's tether,
Chewed through to free him and so rescue
Their beloved friend. He marvelled at her,
Saying, 'I put my trust in both of you,
Strength and stamina I have from Cadair
Beauty and brains are your gift to me,
What can I give back? I promise that
Forever you have my heart and loyalty.'
Then in quiet companionship the trio
Continued on their way with a humbler
Sir Rhydian than first left Castell Du
Learning more as they journey farther.

Treasure Found

Walking down the mountainside they passed several streams
Very straight, with stony sides. This caused Rhydian to
    ponder,
Likening them to the mill leats at home, but there were no
    mills
To be seen. Along each course were pools, becoming broader,
Then narrow again until they joined the meandering river.
They soon reached the water meadows, lush green grass
For Cadair, coneys for Cyfaill to chase, and the sun's warmth
Enticing a weary, chastened, traveller to stay in this serene
    place.
Placing all their belongings on the ground, Rhydian sat down
    to rest.
He took out the leather pouch, and gently drew from it a
    small
Lump of metal, covered in earth, then more, some very
    large.
Lastly he brought out a circlet, with a round stone, rather
    dull,
In the middle. Curious he took them to the water and
    washing
The mud away, a brightness began to show. A sudden dart
Of gold, the circlet caught the light, reflected it back, blue
    fire
Dancing and shimmering from deep within the stone's heart.
As he held it out over the river, he saw the lovely face
    again,
The circlet appeared to nestle in her black hair, her eyes
The same blue as the jewel, opened wide with delight.
He could hear laughter on the wind. He felt no surprise
But a sense of belonging, as if he was looking at a part

Of himself, the kindred soul of a long-known friend.
He gazed down into the water, their eyes entwined.
Slowly the face faded away leaving its imprint in his mind.

The Old Man

Rhydian left Cadair free to graze, no need of tether
Nor hobble, certain he would stay waiting for him.
Calling Cyfaill he took his sling, silken net and dagger
To hunt for supper. The woods nearby beckoned
With promise of a different kind of game to seek.
The trees closed around him, animal tracks crossed
His path, in excitement he saw it, the twrch's unique
Print, stealthily he followed the trail, signs of a group
With young. Suddenly Cyfaill stood still, ears pricked
Nose quivering, she darted off, into the dense bushes.
Curious, Rhydian went after, her way clearly marked,
Unusually, for she was well trained to be a quiet hunter
Who left little trace. He heard her call to him, urgent,
Quickening his pace he found her at a small entrance
Set into the side of the hill. Warily he looked in, bent
Almost double he saw that it opened out, light coming in
From above, a large hound, hackles raised, stood guard.
Cyfaill entered the tunnel, Rhydian, taking out his dagger
Crept after her. He watched her circle, finding it hard
To keep still, but trusting her instincts, he waited.
The great dog let her come close, and tail lifting high
He allowed Rhydian to move forward, there he saw
Movement in the dim recesses and heard a low sigh.
As his eyes grew accustomed he made out the figure
Of an old man, lying on a pile of rags. Using soft words
He drew closer, soothing the hound with his calm voice,
Until he reached the bed. A face, such as an ancient bard's,
Stared up at him, he noted many lines, etched by pain,
A long grey beard below a long narrow nose, with eyes
Of a brighter blue than he had ever seen, much younger
Than the face they dwelt in, yet seeming so old and wise.
Kneeling beside the old man he put his hand on the brow

28

Which felt hot, but dry as if the fever was still to break.
Soaking a cloth from clear water that ran from a spring
In the corner of the cave, willing the old man to speak,
He bathed his face and trickled drops into his mouth.
Stripping back the bedding, as he had seen his mother do,
He wiped the body, freshening and cooling it. He saw
The eyes begin to focus on him, and from the face a new
Light glowed. The eyes closed and he fell into a natural
  sleep.

Parting

For the next five days and long nights Rhydian tended
To the old man, keeping him dry, warm and well fed,
Only leaving the cave to hunt with Cyfaill and visit Cadair.
Health restored from the care given to him by this stranger,
The old man watched from his bed wondering about the
   youth.
He began asking questions about him, seeking to find the truth,
Receiving back a true account. Then answers he was sought.
In quiet companionship they talked throughout the night.
On the next day they parted, to follow their separate ways.
'Sir Rhydian of Castell Du I bid you farewell, these days
Together have brought me joy, I know that we will meet again
For our fates are surely entwined, you cared for me without
   gain.
I am known by different names, if you need me ask for Emrys.
I give you a token, my friends will honour you for bearing
   this.'
Holding the old man in his arms Rhydian felt a hot bolt that
   sped
Between them, curling around his very soul. With tears unshed
He turned and left, Cyfaill, saddened to leave Cabal, the
   wolfhound,
Followed behind. Reunited with Cadair they journeyed on,
   bound
Northward along the river's edge, finding there was an empty
   space
Now lying in his heart, where an old man had claimed his
   own place.

The Gifts

They crossed the river by the old bridge,
Cadair, eager to go after his long rest,
Raced across, giving Rhydian no time
To linger hoping, by the water, afraid lest
She was there, yet afraid she was gone
For evermore. The early morning sun
Lit up the path ahead, like an arrow
Its course was straight. Partly hidden
It climbed out of the valley to the hills
Above, where it made a visible scar,
A white road over the wild moorland.
Into this remote land they travelled, far
From any settlement, to guide them
Nothing but the sun by day and at night
The stars. Rhydian thought of the old man
And his parting gifts, with love and delight.
A cup and ring, made from the same blue
Flecked stone, carved with an ancient sign.
'Wear the ring to show you are my friend,
Drink from the cup if you are in malign
Health or injured, it has the power to cure
The body and the soul if the user is a true
Believer in its worth and uses its power wisely
With no thought of gain. My last gift to you
Is a simple crwth and bow, care for it well,
It was made from the thorn tree of Aramethea.
The music it plays will heal a troubled spirit,
Bring comfort to the grieving and remove fear
From all who hear it, play it well, for my sake.'
They journeyed on for two days, along the high
Road, at night Rhydian sang as he played the crwth,
With music flowing so freely, as if released by

31

The bow from long captivity. On the second day
They came down from the hills to a wide valley
With small houses scattered alongside the river.
As he approached, children came out to see
The stranger and admire his horse and hound,
Pointing at his crwth they chanted Sing, Sing.
Smiling, Rhydian began to play, and as his voice
Gathered in strength the very hills began to ring.

Untouched

The three companions continued the next day
Having sung and talked until the early hours
Of the morning, then on sweet smelling hay
They slept till long past the dawn breaking.
Taking with him new songs and tales,
Rhydian once more travelled northwards
His mind busy with the music and fables
Of last night. As the sun rose high in the sky
Getting warm and lacking sleep, beginning
To feel drowsy, he stopped at a quiet spot,
Lying down on the grass, was soon sleeping.
He was woken by Cyfaill, a low growl
Shaking her body. Sitting on the river bank
Was a slim figure, long black hair falling
Down her back. As he watched, his eyes sank
Into her beauty, slowly he arose and walked
Towards her, as he drew close she raised
Her hand to stop him. 'Come no further,
The time is not yet right.' Then as he gazed
A mist arose from the water, shrouding
Her from view. It cleared and she was gone,
In silence she came and in silence she left.
He searched for signs, but there were none.
Sadly he mounted and continued along the path.

The Fort

They continued alongside the river till nightfall,
Making camp inside one of many ruined buildings
With the grass growing between the stone wall.
Rhydian looked across the river to a small village,
With its church sitting on the top of a low mound.
He remembered the stories told to him yesterday,
Of the place that St Dewi preached, where he found
The skill of oration that lifted him above all others,
The Archbishops' crown was given there, at Brefi.
That night dreams returned to Rhydian, wakening
Him, as the moon shone over the land, he could see
No ruins, but now a fort stood in its place, soldiers,
In full regalia, stood guard along the battlements.
He looked for his two friends, but they had vanished.
With a growing sense of awe and wonderment
He drew nearer. A horseman rode past, so close
He felt the air stir around him, but there was no sound
From any part, no voices, no hooves clattering
Over the flagstones, a deathly silence, so profound
It could almost be heard. A sudden movement
Came from behind him, there he saw two men
Pushing a young, frightened, girl to the ground.
Without a thought, dagger in his hand, Sir Rhydian
Charged, ready to battle for the maiden's honour.
He ran straight through them, making no contact,
The figures wavered, as if blown by a waft of air,
The girl broke free, running fast. Slow to react
The two men could not catch her, in bad humour
They returned to the fort. The girl turned round
A puzzled look in her deep blue eyes, her long hair,
Black as the night, framed her face. Rhydian frowned
For she was his water sprite, yet could not see him.

34

As he stood watching, the dawn broke, sweeping
Away the fort, the girl, the soldiers. Once more
Rhydian could see Cadair and Cyfaill, still sleeping
Peacefully amongst the broken, ruined walls.

Aldan

Rhydian looked to the hills beyond the ruins,
Where the old road marched on, straight as a lance,
Heading Northwards. He had followed this track
For many miles, yet now felt a strange reluctance
To follow the same route any more. With a new
Yearning he took the pathway down to the river,
Where a deep ford crossed over to the village,
To the place where St Dewi had come to deliver
His oration against the heretics, the followers of
Pelagius. On reaching the small hill he climbed
Up to the church and entered with a sense of awe
And reverence. As he approached the half timbered
Chancel he could feel a passion trapped within
Its very walls. Closing his eyes, he opened his mind
Willing the spirit shadows to reveal their secrets.
Waiting in stillness across the centuries, hoping to find
Answers to, as yet, unformed and unasked questions.
The cool dim interior seemed to be bathed in light,
The silence broken by an angelic voice, softly at first
Then growing louder. To the new young knight
It felt as if his soul was being lifted by the beauty
Of a sound, that was both strange yet well known.
As he slowly turned to face its source, all faded
Away, leaving not a note behind, as if blown
By the mountain breeze, scattered into the air.
Yet there did remain a trace, a glowing ember,
Hidden deep, warming his being from within,
For it was the very essence of life. Feeling humbler
He left the church and rode towards the village green.
Here people were selling their wares, cloth, bread,
Chickens in cages, pens with piglets, squealing loudly
Children poked them with sticks laughing, as they fled

From side to side. Rhydian looked with longing at the
Loaves, realising how boring a diet of fish and coney
Can be. He picked up his cwrth and began to play,
Ballads and love songs that flowed as sweet as honey.
A crowd gathered around him as he started singing.
His voice at first caressing, soft and gentle, gradually
Rising in strength to a final, soaring crescendo
Reaching to all those listening, even across the valley.
There was a moment of silence when he finished,
Then a mighty wave of applause, coins were tossed
At his feet and he was almost swept along the street
By the throng of admirers. Still smiling, he crossed
To the bakers stand, now with money to buy plenty.
As he wandered around the market he heard barking
From the green, turning he saw one man with raised stick
Aimed at Cyfaill, another man, with Cadair's reins, trying
To lead him away. Rhydian shouted in great anger and ran
Straight at them. With a parting kick at the hound the men
Disappeared. 'Your fine horse can be a great temptation,
You need to guard him well; these parts are a thieves den.'
A pair of bright blue eyes looked at Rhydian, for a moment
His heart leapt, but the face they were set in was older
Than his maiden from last night, her black hair was flecked
With grey, her figure yet still trim, and the stare colder.
'If you are travelling alone keep to the open road and trust
None.' Rhydian, thanking her for the advice, asked her name.
'I am called Aldan, I see you are wearing the ring of Emrys
For that I give you help.' Saying no more she passed him,
Entering a small house. Rhydian thought carefully, for his
Cadair was a noble destrier and that could not be hidden.
He must take care now he was travelling along well used
Routes. He would keep watch and as he had been bidden
Trust no one. With a heavy heart he continued on his way.

Part Two
In
Friendship

An Unexpected Companion

Rhydian took the valley road out of Brefi,
Other travellers were also journeying,
With goods and livestock, both in company
And alone. Keeping a good distance behind
Them he rode thoughtfully along, wondering
Which pathway to follow, the gentle low road
Much frequented, with the fears that might bring,
Or once more to take the high ground, to the hills
Where the very wildness itself brought danger.
It was not far to the next settlement, and the sun
Was warm on his back, the river road pleasanter
Than climbing to the sparse moorlands above.
He lunched by the water, Cyfaill chasing stones
Thrown for her by Rhydian, who thought about
The tales he had heard at Brefi, of old crones,
Wizards and enchantresses, of daring deeds
And stories from days past. He then weaved
These into songs, strumming his crwth creating
Melodies, softly singing until he believed
They were worthy to be heard. Decided on his
Course he continued once more along the road,
Continuing through the village without halting
Until he came to where the valley became broad.
A vast bog stretched in front of him where once
A lake had been. Watchful of his step he kept
In the lee of the hills, where the ground was firm.
Rising above, small hillocks, as if dragons slept
Amidst a cauldron of mire. Not trusting the ground
Beneath him, Cadair trod carefully, picking his way
Along ancient paths. That night they heard strange
Eerie calls, spirit fires dancing, Ellylldan's at play.
Morning broke, waking Rhydian from restless slumber,

All around was peaceful, a layer of mist hanging like
A blanket over the land. A rustle in the reeds caused
Him to turn quickly, there lying in a small dyke,
Was a boy, with black hair and deep blue eyes
A face so familiar to Rhydian he felt no surprise
At finding him in this remote place. Taking his hand
He pulled the urchin out, and surveyed his prize.
'Tell me, son of Aldan, why you have followed me,
And what is your name?' The boy stared at Rhydian,
'How do you know who I am? My name is Alain,
My mother charged me with tracking you, hidden,
To watch for any danger until it was safe to show
Myself – but I fell into the bog and now you will
Send me home.' He looked shamed, but stood tall
And straight, and although his eyes began to fill
His gaze did not waver. 'Your eyes told me who
You are. Your courage too. If you wish to come
With me a while I will be glad of your company.'
The boy flushed with pride, then he drew from
Inside his coat a parcel, which he gave to Rhydian.
'This is a gift for you, from my mother.' The gift
Was very soft and light, a blanket woven from fine
Yarn, with many shades of blue, grey-blue of mist
To the deep blue of night, it seemed to shimmer
In the sunlight capturing the warmth and reflecting
Its light. His hands felt a glow spreading over his body.
'My mother sends this to keep you from any chilling
Of the spirit, as well as keeping the cold at bay, you
Will be refreshed whenever you use this for cover,
An hour's sleep will be as a full night. She has only
Woven one other.' Feeling its touch, gentle as a lover
Rhydian was overcome. 'She gave this to me, a stranger?'
Alain smiled, 'She said you were known to her, how
I have no knowledge.' Twisting Emrys' ring he knew
This was truth, a thread bound them and he made a vow
That before his journey ended he would seek the answer.

Singing For Their Supper

As the sun rose, burning the mist from the land,
Over the river, meandering through its flood plain.
A lonely scene, stretching as far as Rhydian could see.
On all sides, as the flat peat mire ended, a mountain
Rose steeply upwards, with the sun's reflected rays
Creating a circle of fire. Shadowy demons chased
Across the valley, fading into the dawning light.
He was reluctant to leave, for magical spirits graced
This place and there was a sense of belonging, as if
He had been here before. He knew the ways, untold,
How to avoid the deep quaking pits, where to tread
To find the solid ground beneath his feet, with old
Understanding, passed to him from lives gone by.
Alain looked expectantly at him, unsure of his place,
Ready to go, he almost quivered with excitement.
Rhydian smiled as he looked at the eager young face,
'It seems I have acquired a squire of my own,
Strange, only a few days since, that was my role.'
They travelled slowly, for Cadair found the way hard,
Sinking in the moss he struggled to gain control
In the marsh, using his great strength he forced
A pathway through. Cyfaill found the going easy
She seemed to glide over the reed beds, leaving
No trace behind. Turning eastwards, under the lee
Of the hills, where the ground rose higher, a track
Took them safely over the land. Here were workings,
Where peat had been dug out for the fires of houses
Scattered along the edge, on the hillside, clearings,
Making patchworks of green set among the brown.
Alain spoke to Rhydian, 'Ahead is a town with fairs
Where many visit, they have jugglers and games.
I come here, with my mother, who sells her wares.

I earn coins by holding horses and running errands.'
In truth, now he had two to feed and needed bread.
Looking at the boy's face, with his bright blue eyes
Shining, he could not gainsay him, laughing he said
"As my squire you must only attend to my horse."
At this Rhydian vaulted up onto Cadair's broad back,
Pulling Alain up behind him, they left Cors Carron's
Treacherous paths to follow the white monks' track.
In high humour they rode into the small town,
Passing other travellers on their way to the fair.
Alain led them to an inn where he was known,
There he sought shelter from the cool night air
In the warm dry stable loft, as so often before.
Rhydian settled Cadair on fresh straw, filled the rick
With sweet smelling hay, and left him with Cyfaill
For company. Alain watched, keen to be quick
To learn his new duties. A Celtic stone cross
Marked the site where the fair was to be held,
The cobbled square already taking on a festive
Air. In a field adjacent were brightly coloured
Flags fluttering from poles, and in the middle
Was a raised dais, whilst at the far end, a row
Of Butts was being erected. Looking around
He felt a wave of excitement beginning to grow
Inside him, for this was no ordinary village fair.
The pair returned to the inn full of the sights
With much to ask Alain's friends. In past visits
Alain worked as pot boy, paying for his night's
Lodging, with two hungry boys, a horse and dog
'Twas not enough. The Innkeeper, seeing Rhydian's
Crwth, asked him what manner of songs he played,
Not monkish chants or lovesick ballads, his guests'
Tastes were for an altogether more bawdy fare.
Alain washed and Rhydian sang for their keep

That night, until they tumbled into their beds
Tired but happy, ready for a good nights sleep
To prepare themselves for the morrow's fair.

The Fair Day

In the early morning light, Rhydian crept quietly down
To the stable, not wishing to disturb his new friend,
With only a halter he rode Cadair away from the town.
None had yet risen, with the only sounds to be heard
Those of animals in their pens and of vermin scuttling
Through the deserted streets. They cantered through
The water meadows, he could feel his horse stretching
Himself, enjoying the freedom after a night indoors.
As people began to stir he turned back for the inn
Where he found Alain had prepared a fresh straw bed
For Cadair, and with Cyfaill's head on his knee, sitting
By a newly cleaned saddle. Rhydian gathered up
All their possessions, which he carefully stowed
In a corner of the stable, well hidden in the straw.
Leaving the horse and hound behind they strode
Out of the courtyard, crwth slung over his shoulder,
They made for the market where many tradesmen
Were setting up stalls, hassling for the best places,
And amongst them, bartering had already begun.
They bought marchpane and honey sweetmeats
From a pedlar, washed down with a cup of beer.
They turned to the tourney field, where preparations
Were underway for the combat games. A loud jeer
From behind caused him to turn, a group of men
Were laughing at him and pointing to his crwth.
'Sing us a love song, pretty boy, we are wrestlers,
Travelled from Cornwall, to win prizes, a youth
Such as you, with golden hair and soft white skin
Can pleasure us, if no maidens can be found.'
Feeling anger rise inside him, though struggling
To keep calm, Rhydian passed them, not a sound

Did he utter, instead he headed for the booths
And placed his name to all the lists, taking part
In every game, from quarter staves and archery
To stone pitching and tug o'war. Then, his heart
Racing, he added his mark to the main attraction.

The Games

With still some hours before the games started
The two wandered around the fair, mingling with
The jugglers. As Rhydian sang, a crowd collected,
While they listened to him silence fell, people
Stopped their work until he finished singing,
Then they resumed, spirits uplifted, pockets
Lighter, the beauty of his voice still ringing
In their ears. A band marched through the fair,
Leading the drummers, a small dancing dog
Twirled to his piper as they wended their way
To the games. A hand cart with the greased hog
Was pushed by a small boy, who puffed his way
To the field. Rhydian attached himself to the rear
Of this motley crew, carrying the crwth. Alain
Followed, his excitement tinged with a fear
That his new friend might have overstepped
Himself. On the field Rhydian found the tents,
Alain counted his money, there was plenty
For the side shows, first he bet clipped pence
At the cock pit. He climbed the greasy pole,
Chased the greased pig, and threw horseshoes
At rings. His cock won and he caught the pig,
He slithered up the pole, seeming unable to lose,
His pile of pennies grew. Gleefully he went to
The Archery Butts to watch as Rhydian started
His games. Many years of practice gave him
True flight, finding the bullseye with repeated
Shafts. The fighting with staves had an extra
Part, taking place on a large log, balancing
Over a muddy pond. Roars of laughter could
Be heard for whenever one of those fighting

Lost their balance they fell into the quagmire.
Being quite light and lithe this was one sport
Rhydian had loved as a boy, his nimble feet
And natural balance kept him steady as he fought
All comers. As he progressed around the field
His support grew, until he reached the centre,
Where the Cornish wrestlers waited for him.
Alain looked at the slight figure of his mentor
Measuring up against his burly opponents,
A great fear gnawed away at his inside
He would be hurt, injured, perhaps maimed
For life, or worse, and all for an injured pride.
The men from Kernow reigned supreme
On the field of combat, throwing with ease
All challengers, until their champion, as yet
Untroubled, within his grasp the tourneys
Prize, met the last man to fight. A stripling
In borrowed garb, who appeared no threat
To the thickset, swarthy wrestler. Gleefully
He beckoned him closer, to accept his defeat.
As the two men circled each other the crowd
Became still. They held the loose linen tunics
Each tried to pull the other down. Experience
Versus youth, a solid rock against acrobatics.
Unable to hold this slippery adversary for long,
With patience being tried by quick sharp kicks,
His temper began to rise he dropped his guard.
Using unexpected strength, Rhydian attacks.
The older man hits the ground there he stays
Down, for the allotted time, with head bowed
Unable to rise, he submits, relinquishing his
Crown. Rising to its feet the cheering crowd
Give their homage to a new Champion.

49

The Aftermath

With the cheers of the crowd ringing in his ears
Rhydian felt himself being lifted up, high in the air
Onto the broad shoulders of the men from Kernow,
Who paraded him around the field, with not a care
For the loser. Stripping the borrowed wrestling tunic
From his lithe body, they left him bare to the waist,
Creating lustful pleasure among the young maids,
With those older wishing their years had not haste
By so quickly, whilst in this heady excitement
The defeated man slipped unnoticed from the ground.
After some time the victor and his squire left the fair,
Alain carrying a squealing, greasy, piglet, fat and round,
Rhydian, the winner's purse and a linen tunic given to
    him
As a memento of this day. Neither saw the movement
Behind them, a shadowy figure, keeping distance,
Following them, watching which way they went.
At the inn they checked on Cadair, a gentle whinny
Greeting them, they released Cyfaill from her long wait
Then promising to return very soon, went into the inn.
A figure silently entered the stable, eyes alight with hate
Bent on revenge, he saw a richer prize than he had lost.
And softly he approached Rhydian's beloved horse.
The inn was very noisy as revellers packed inside, beer
Flowed freely, tales told, becoming increasingly coarse.
Cyfaill suddenly sprang up, hackles raised, barking loudly,
Rhydian followed across the yard, with pounding heart
He reached the stall. Cadair stood still, nostrils flaring
Sweat breaking out down his neck, legs braced apart.
In the gloom, slumped against the wall, with blood
Pouring from his head, breathing laboured, uneven,
All colour drained away, lay the defeated wrestler.

Rhydian bent down and gently moved him. It was then
He saw the damaged leg, badly smashed and twisted.
Calling for Alain to fetch his saddle pack, he withdrew
Emrys' cup, filling it with water from Cadair's trough
He bathed the head wound. The ice cold water grew
Warmer as it touched the skin, inducing a healing
Sleep to settle on the injured man, then covering him
In Aldan's blanket Rhydian, worried, left him to sleep.
'I can care for his head wound, but his broken limb
Is beyond my knowledge. The monks at Ystrad Fflur
Can tend him well, so tonight I must take him there.'
Alain started to argue, he could not understand why
This man should not be left, why this concern and care
For a thief. Looking stern Rhydian replied 'Judge no man
For we are no better than our fellows. I have vowed
To serve all those in need and in this I will not falter.'
Alain was humbled by these words, and felt proud
To follow such a knight. 'Give me your commands
For I am your squire until the sun sets on eternity.'
A simple litter was made using the two linen tunics
Threaded through wooden staves, on which to carry
The man over the rough road high into the mountains.
Gathering all their belongings they bade the innkeeper
Farewell and set off into the darkening night, Rhydian
Walking beside the litter, pulled by a reluctant Cadair,
Alain sitting on his back, with Cyfaill leading the way.

The Abbey

They walked non-stop throughout the night
Reaching the Abbey as the bell tolled
For prime. One monk, seeing their plight,
Took them to the infirmary, uttering
No words he indicated that they enter.
The room was light and airy, with the scent
Of rosemary pervading the air, clear water
Bubbled from a spring, filling a stone trough
In the dispensary. Laying his charge on a bed
Rhydian spoke to the monk. 'I believe this man
Was injured by my horse, I have travelled
Overnight to bring him into your care. His
Head wound I have cleaned, I ask you to set
His leg, this I cannot do, neither have I the skill
In herbs to reduce his fever. I will be in your debt
If you will help him.' Looking at the young man
The monk broke silence. 'My assistant is at the fair
I will need someone with strength and courage
For this work.' 'Give me but two hours to prepare
Myself and I will be your aide.' Then replacing
Aldan's blanket with another he found a place
To sleep, leaving Cadair's care to Alain. Dreams
Came quickly to him, colours swirl through space
Merging into shapes which create a landscape.
Nine maidens bathe in the water of a blue lake
They beckon to the dreamer, enticing him to
Join them. At his approach two figures forsake
The others, then, offering him food and drink
They lead him to the shore and sit him down
On a bed of soft rushes, covering him in flowers.
The dark-haired maiden spreads her lace gown
Around her as she kneels beside the dreamer

With her fair-haired companion on his other side.
Two pairs of eyes, one of the deepest blue,
The other, bright as the summer sky, open wide
With pleasure as they caress his body, anointing
Him with salves, bringing comfort to his weary
Limbs. A mist rises up from the water, deepening
Until all vanish from sight. Waking, after barely
An hour's rest, feeling refreshed and with a sense
Of purpose, Rhydian returned to the bedside
Where the monk had gathered his herbs and
Tools for the work ahead, for this he was untried
And prayed for strength and courage in his task.

Brother Thomas

In a quiet corner of the Abbey courtyard
Rhydian sat alone, listening to the plain chant
Of Vespers, gathering his thoughts after a hard,
Long, day. His mind went back to his sleep
That morning, still feeling the soothing hands
Of the two maids, unknown, but who were to him
Achingly familiar. Still further back, to the demands
Of the long nights journey, when it seemed as if
His charge would not be with them by daybreak.
He pondered on the reviving powers that came
With the stone cup, for it could be seen to make
The pain easier to bear, keeping the fever at bay,
Yet it was only water, drawn from a mountain nant.
He dwelt on the look of hate and loathing cast
On him by the injured man, as if it would haunt
Him for all-time. He drew his blanket around him,
Once more gaining peace from the softly woven
Cloth, as if love itself was giving him protection
From the world. Had the same magic driven
The hate from his opponent's heart during the
Journey? Or did it choose whom it would serve?
His mind went forward to the day's happenings
The admiration he had for the skill and nerve
Of the healer had grown throughout the day.
He felt a desire in himself to acquire the same
Knowledge, to have in his hands the ability
To heal, to preserve life, not to lay claim
To another's in combat. His mind was in conflict
With the training he had received since childhood.
He felt a shadow fall across him, as Brother Thomas,
The Infirmerer, walked towards him, then stood
Quietly, looking down with a gentle concern.

'May I join you here?' he asked 'I believe you
May be troubled and I would like to offer my help
If you so desire.' 'You do indeed speak true,
I doubt my chosen path. I would like to stay here
With you, in this newly endowed Abbey, to learn
Your skills, to spend my hours in contemplation
Exchanging thoughts with the brothers, and yearn
To be a part of this community.' Thomas replied
Gravely 'I would dearly like to keep you, I know
That soon my time will come, and if I can teach
You well I would go happy that you will follow
In my ways. But you have much to consider first,
This life is a hard one, much of men's pleasures
Are denied to us, the love of a woman, the joy
Of seeing one's firstborn son, worldly treasures
Are not ours, you are as yet young and untried.'
Rhydian raised his eyes, uncertainty and pain
Reaching out to the older man. 'What must I do?
How to choose which way to go, can I not remain
Here with you?' Thomas looked sternly back
'Remember, you have promised your lord,
The Prince Llewellyn, to travel to Castell y Bere.
To join his retinue, a life you have not abhorred
Till now. I charge you to continue on your quest.'
Then he rested his hand on Rhydian's shoulder,
'Be not afraid, all will become clear to you soon,
There are many routes that lead to the answer
You seek, I will pray for you to receive guidance
From a higher authority than me.' At this he
Turned away. Rhydian reflected on all that had
Passed, then he made a decision, a way to see
Where his future should lie. With this he lay down
Under the starlit sky, his blanket wrapping him in
The dreamless sleep that sweetly took away his fears
And frets, finding his strength from deep within.

Decisions To Be Made

With the rising sun lighting the new day
Rhydian searched for Alain, finding him
In the stable, asleep on a soft bed of hay,
Horse and hound curled around the boy.
He turned, leaving them still slumbering
Making his way towards the Infirmary
With the low chant from Matins filling
His mind. Brother Thomas greeted him,
Leading the way towards a low bed.
'Our friend had a restful night, he tells
Me his name is Ythel, from Lys Kerwyd,
He wishes to speak to you, I told him of
Your journey, he feels that he is beholden
In this, it does not sit easy on such as he.'
The man stirred and looking at Rhydian
Tried to speak, but his voice was so low
Rhydian had to strain to catch his words.
'I had such hatred in my heart for you,
I tried to steal your horse for my rewards,
Yet you brought me here, gave assistance
To the good brother without any thought
Of gain. It is beyond my understanding.'
His brow was furrowed as he sought
To find the reasons. 'Do not strive for
Answers, you needed help, this I gave.
Sleep now, when you wake I will be gone.'
Ythel spoke again, 'Before you go I crave
That you will talk with me once more, when
I have regained my strength.' Rhydian sighed,
'So be it, I will return again before nightfall
Now be at ease.' Knowing that he must decide
To leave the abbey, it would be hard to linger

56

For his resolve may yet weaken, then together
With Brother Thomas he went to the refectory.
Alain eagerly greeted him, 'I wondered whether
Morpheus would have claimed you for all of today.'
Rhydian smiled, gaining pleasure from his bright
Face. Cyfaill crept under his seat, resting her head
On his knee, he could feel her body pressing tight
Against him. A rush of pure love ran through him
For all he held dear, could he leave these for a new
Path to take? He felt confused, he needed time alone,
He would talk with Alain later, for now he drew
Breath and kept his thoughts and plans close.

The Dream Hawk

Whilst it was still dark Rhydian crept silently
Down to the stable to say goodbye to Cadair,
Cyfaill trying to follow, was turned back.
'Twill not be for long my friends, I am eager
To leave before day breaks, look after Alain,
I trust you.' With that he picked up his pack
And slipped quietly out of the Abbey grounds,
Heading northwards he took the old track
Into the high mountains. With birds greeting
The new day, Rhydian joined the dawn song
Letting his voice soar high on the wind
Taking with it the tension of the long
Days past. The climb upwards was steep,
Rhydian revelled in the hard walk, feeling
His body working, numbing his mind.
Reaching the top he stopped, looking
Backwards to the Abbey, half hidden
By trees he could see the garden, visible
As a patch of green among the grey stones.
He sat down on the grass, enjoying the simple
Pleasure of silence, nothing to disturb him
But the wind, birds and his own thoughts.
He recalled Ythel's words when they talked
Last night. There would be no more fights
For him, but he had found peace within
The abbey, and for as long as he desired,
He was welcome to stay as a Lay Brother.
Rhydian had given the winnings acquired
At the fight to Ythel, to pay for his keep
Until he could work, he knew that instead
Of an enemy, he had found a true friend,

Who valued the peace that now replaced
The turmoil and the loneliness of his past.
Before he remembered she was not there,
Rhydian put out his hand, feeling for Cyfaill.
His mind went to Alain, the burden of care
Placed on him rested heavy on his young
Shoulders, yet this was tempered by pride
At the trust given to him. He would travel
To the Mynach river, journeying alongside
The abbey workmen, to the Devil's bridge,
To wait for Rhydian to join him. In the warm
Sun and the peaceful quiet, Rhydian slept.
The gentle breeze caressed him, no harm
Or troublesome thoughts disturbing him.
In his sleep he became a hawk who flew
Over land and sea, swooping down beside
A lake, where, with an eye so keen and true
He plucked a fish from the water, holding
It in his sharp talons, settling on a stony
Crag to eat his feast. From this lofty perch
He viewed the hills and moors, the beauty
Painted in wide brush stokes onto a natural
Canvas. As he watched, the water stirred
In the middle of the lake, creating a wave
That flowed to the shore, there it crashed
Into foam, the water receding, revealing
A young woman, clad in a simple shift
Coloured with all the blues and greens
Of the skies and seas, head bowed, a gift
From the water gods. A young man came
Towards her, hands outstretched in greeting
Enfolding him in her embrace they stood
In silence, so close, with their hearts beating
As one. The man looked upwards, the face
Of young Emrys watched the Rhyd-Hawk,

Smiling as if he knew whose soul the dream
Bird carried. Slowly the pair began to walk
Into the water until they had disappeared
From sight. The Hawk, gathering speed
Flew northwards, until moving so fast
All became a blur, nothing could impede
The heedless flight. As they slowed down
The land spread below them, jutting out
Into the sea, there plying its way across
A narrow rocky passage, sailed a small boat.
Three women were weeping over the still
Form of a man. They were heading for
An island, steered by a man with long hair
And a grey flowing beard, waiting ashore
For them, a group of monks, with litter ready
To receive the wounded man and convey
Him to the island monastery. Stepping out
Of the boat, the old man looked up at the sky.
Emrys smiled and saluted the circling Hawk.
With a sudden start Rhydian awoke, still
In a dreamlike trance, he gathered his wits
He felt the wind on his face, the thrill
Of the flight remaining deep within him.
Once more taking the hidden pathways
Over the mountains, he wondered about
The dream and especially of the Fayes,
Who inhabited those watery places.

The Decision Made

Rhydian looked at the hard terrain
He had to traverse. Deep valleys cut
Into the hillsides, with the high plain
Windswept and bare, there was no
Shelter to be found. No habitation
To seek refuge in on stormy nights.
Lonely, with nature asking a question
Of the traveller. Had he the physical
Power required as well as the inner
Strength needed? Clearing his mind
Of the petty debris that could hinder
The thinking that he so much needed,
Then, with one last backwards glance,
He strode out. Keeping the sun to his
Right, he went, straight as a lance,
Over the beautiful, forbidding hills.
He found water, fast running, clear
And cool, he took shelter in green
Valley meadows, with sheep, deer
And the wild black cattle grazing
Beside him. His thoughts chased
Around his head, creating a never
Ending circle of doubts to be faced
Before any decisions could be made.
In the quiet, music came unbidden
To him, songs of love, hymns of
Praise. Emotions, often hidden
Inside, took hold and drowned
Him with their power. At night
Sleep came easily, renewing him
By daybreak, when the sun's light
Woke him to his thoughts again.

Soon his journey's end was close,
He could see the river far below,
Now was the time for him to choose
Between the abbey and contentment,
Or the world and all the heartache
It brings. The time alone had been
Welcome, now he knew the way to take.
Standing by the bridge that spanned
The treacherous river, a boy and hound
Kept watch, as they did every day.
The dog suddenly sprang with a bound,
Giving tongue, she ran up the narrow
Path, the boy followed, hope rising.
In the distance, arms outstretched
Ran another boy, his voice calling
Them, he knelt down as the hound
Reached him, eyes bright with tears
He waited for his young friend.
Gone forever his doubts and fears,
He knew now where his future lay.

Alain's Tale

Crossing the narrow bridge that spanned the river
Rhydian was filled with admiration for the plucky
Men who had built it across the high narrow gorge
Of the Mynach, where ferns grew from the rocky
Walls, drenched by water cascading down the falls.
The stable yard close by, Cadair, hearing a beloved
Voice, whinnied loudly, restless until he felt a hand
Running along his side, an arm on his neck, pressed
Into his warm coat, Rhydian, full with tears of love
Welling up inside his heart. *'I will not leave you again
That is my promise, we will all face the world together.'*
He slept well that night, no dreams or visions came
To disturb him, waking refreshed, ready for the next
Part of his journey. This was a hard route to traverse,
Over wild mountains where wolves may yet be found.
With need to travel swiftly and safely over the adverse
Terrain. Now, to Alain's delight, he rode his own horse,
A sturdy cob, nimble, well used to the mountain paths.
They kept to the river's edge, climbing steadily passing
Lonely farmsteads, where smoke rose from the hearths
Until they reached the lowest slopes of the hills, here
There was still shelter, lush grazing and game to hunt,
They made their camp, baking freshly caught trout
In the ashes of their fire. As the flames grew dormant
Alain began to talk, hesitantly at first, as if afraid
To open his deepest thoughts. 'I have often caught
The wild ponies at home, then ridden them till being
Thrown, but never before has such a gift been bought
For me. I will cherish her for ever, I shall call her
Bronn, after my father – and my brother.' Alain tried
To stem a tear, and remained silent for a while, then
In a low voice he continued 'As a child I would hide

When my mother was sad, as she often was, she would
Sit for long hours gazing into the river by our home,
My sister would care for me, though but a child herself.
We would have days of freedom, where we could roam
The hills unhindered. Then one day that all ceased, Mam
Kept us close by, afraid lest we strayed out of her calling.
Gwendydd, my sister, told me stories as I grew older, how
Our father had taken Bron with him on a journey, following
The Prince Madoc to distant lands. Mam begged him not
To take Bron, but to no avail. They shared the gift I lack,
Of seeing each other when by water, she could watch him
And know all was well. She knew they would not come back,
That my father died, so Bron grew to manhood on distant
Shores, then one day she saw him no more. That was when
Our carefree hours finished for a time. Then, one day sitting
By the river, looking as always deep into the water, Gwen
Saw, among strange animals, a young boy, with bare, dark
Skin. She called to Mam, and the two stared, quite intent
For a while, looking into the water, then with a long sigh
Mam went indoors. From that day she was more content
To let us wander, as long as we stayed together, but Gwen
Was sent away, to my Lord Llewyllyn's castle, to be taught
The ways of a lady. I could no longer go alone, she knew
I had not the sight.' Alain paused for breath. 'I thought
It strange when told, ere you arrived, that I would soon be
Travelling with a knight. Mam was watching for your arrival
She knew who you were, what you looked like, and that I
Would be safe with you. She warned me to be heedful
Of strangers, to give you support and take note of your
Chivalry. I believe that you also have the sight, not yet,
Methinks, as keen as Mam's or Gwen's, but sufficient for
Others to watch over you, I give thanks for now I've met
You, and my future and my life have changed forever.'

The Cwm

As they climbed higher the land around
Seemed familiar to Rhydian, yet he had not
Travelled here before. He turned eastwards
To the highest point, eyes seeking the spot
Where the dream Rhyd-Hawk had perched.
'I know that there is a lake up there, I must
Go to see it.' Cadair, feeling his excitement
Broke into a canter, leaving a cloud of dust
For Alain and Cyfaill to follow. At the top
He stopped, gazing down at the dark, cool
Water of the cwm. The sun's rays reflected
Flashes of pure gold dancing over the pool
As if it was on fire. Slowly, he rode down
To the waters edge, there dismounting,
He waited. From a distance Alain kept
Watch and wondered, not understanding
What disturbed his friend, but patiently
Holding back his questions until the time
Was right. After some while Rhydian spoke.
'Can your sister Gwen summon your Mam
To speak to her, or must they just bide by
The water and wait?' 'I know that if Bron
Was in danger or sad, Mam could sense it,
She would sit and wait after he had gone,
Often all day, until she saw him, they did
Not speak. She said that Gwen had more
Strength than her and could command her
From long distances, but I have no power
At all.' He seemed saddened by his lack
Of sight, as if it made him a lesser person.
'Emrys would tell me about his own sister,
Called Gwendydd too, that there was none

Stronger than her. She could be in one place
And when sleeping, would appear elsewhere.
Sometimes I think our Gwen can also do this.'
'Alain, who is Emrys? I have seen him here,
In a dream, you know him well, tell me more.'
'My grandmother died when Mam was a day
Old, Emrys came and took her to live with him.
We call him our Taid, but if he is I cannot say.
He does not age, being always a very old man.'
Rhydian was thoughtful, then with one last look
At the lake he remounted going northwards,
As he had flown when the dream Rhyd-Hawk.

The Fight

The weather was kind to the travellers.
The nights were warm and the days
Glorious sunshine in which to enjoy
The peace and beauty of the place.
They tarried by streams, talked long
Into the night, telling tales of knights
And adventure. Slowly they crossed
The land of five peaks whose heights
Gave birth to five rivers flowing freely
To the seas in their own joyful dance.
During this time Rhydian taught Alain
How to fight with the sword and lance.
Taking his knightly accoutrements out
Of their coverings he showed him how
To dress himself and Cadair, as a squire
Should. The big Destrier did not allow
Anyone other than those he trusted
To place the gaudy trappings on his
Back, but Alain had already gained
His love and he stood, in quietness
Whilst the young boy struggled with
The heavy caparison. As yet no shield
Or mail, these remained at Castell Du.
Just his sword and its tooled scabbard,
Shining brightly with Alain's proud care.
The path over the high peaks led steeply to
The river Dyfi, where small hamlets lay
Along the river as it meandered through
Meadows until reaching the open seas.
Steadily descending they reached shelter
Among the trees, with welcome grazing
And more game to follow than on higher

Ground. Rhydian gently caressed Cyfaill
In the warming glow of the firelight.
'Methinks you eat too well, you get fat!'
Alain laughed, 'For such a clever knight
You know very little! Your hound bitch
Is pregnant, not fat.' Rhydian was shocked
And concerned. 'I must not take her over
Such rough ground, she needs to be cared
For.' Alain asked who the stud dog was.
Rhydian looked blank, for his father
Bred but carefully, no dog from home
Had sired these pups, yet what other?
An image came to mind, that of Cyfaill at
Play with the large wolfhound of Emrys.
He looked in awe at her as she lay asleep
So peacefully. 'Rhydian, you must not fuss
Her now, she is fit and strong and there
Is a while yet before she whelps.' That
Night he slept fitfully, uneasy, he took
His sword and laid one hand on its flat
Blade, the other held the hilt, for he felt
They were being watched by unfriendly
Eyes. The fire died down, the moon was
Hidden by clouds, so shapes could barely
Be seen. The hound's sharp nose and eyes
Alerted Rhydian to figures moving towards
The camp, before he could awaken Alain
They attacked. His long training from lords
Of battle made him react quickly, Cyfaill
Kept one at bay, another held Alain down
A third circled Rhydian, with a large stave
Clasped in his hands. His face was brown
From many years under the sun, his clothes
Were ragged and coarse. For a moment
He felt a shaft of fear run through him,

Then anger, these two created a potent
Mixture, and with a loud roar Sir Rhydian
Fought with all the skill he had learned.
In truth, it did not last long, Cadair came
To Alain's aid and Cyfaill's quarry turned
Quickly, running off. Rhydian cut the stave
In two, knocking the man to the ground,
He lifted his sword up high, ready to strike.
Slowly he lowered his arm, for he found
At the point of victory, he could not take
Another's life. The defeated man lay still
Not daring to move, gripped with fear,
Waiting yet for this young knight to kill.
Rhydian quietly took him by the hand
And lifted him up. 'Go in peace friend
And learn all is not what it may seem.'
Then watched the man as he rejoined
The others in the shelter of the trees.
Alain looked at him strangely, uncertain
What to say. ' Why did you let him go?
He would have killed, had us they beaten.'
 Rhydian answered with a rueful smile
'I know not, I have been taught to fight,
But not to kill, and when I faced reality
I failed. In truth, I felt it was not right,
But was this my conscience or my fear?'

Castell y Bere

He did not sleep again that night
But strummed his crwth singing
Quietly to himself. The music ran
Around Alain's head, soothing
Him, inducing the sleep that
Eluded his friend. The events
Of the night caused Rhydian much
Soul searching, were they portents
For the future? Could he be a true
Knight if he failed in the last act?
Though he did not regret his action
Yet he could not deny its impact.
He longed to talk to someone
To help him wrestle this demon.
He thought of Emrys, or Thomas,
He desired so much the wisdom
Of his father, who had known
Battles yet still desired peace.
He wrapped himself in Aldan's
Blanket, with its welcome release
From stress and gathered his thoughts.
As dawn broke they continued towards
The river, avoiding all houses, taking
The road to the old fort, crossing fords
Over the winding rivers. Rhydian shut
His mind to all visions of water sprites,
Afraid they would weaken his resolve
To travel fast. He must forgo his delights
And follow his liege Lord's directions
Already the journey had taken too long.
From the fort he took the direct route
Over the ridges of high land. A strong

Wind blew in from the sea, heavily
Laden with salt leaving a rich taste
On his tongue, he very much wanted
To go to the shores, but was in haste
So turned his back and rode onward,
Reaching the far side by nightfall.
There he stopped, Castell y Bere
Atop a hill, with a partly built wall
Marking out the extent of the new
Castell. Rhydian was suddenly afeared,
His journey had been an adventure
Now that he had arrived, and neared
The end found he did not want to stay,
Desiring instead to ask many questions.
There were paths to follow, to explore,
A blue-eyed water sprite who beckons
Showing visions and dreams to unravel.
Could he exchange all of that for a life
At court, with trivial pastimes and mock
Fights to pass the time in unreal strife?
He waited quietly for Alain to prepare
Cadair, he put on his tabard, strapped
His sword to his side, then the party
Rode through the gate as Rhydian led
Them to meet the Prince Llewellyn.

71

Part Three
The
Court

The Prince

The new Castell stood on a small hill
The flood plains of two rivers creating
A natural moat on three sides, the fourth
Protected by the mountain side rising
Steeply upwards. Inside the half-built
Stone walls the tower of the unfinished
Keep formed a black silhouette against
The red sky of sunset, its edges burnished
Gold by the dying rays. Passing through
Opened gates, they reached a courtyard
Overflowing with people and animals.
Rhydian dismounted, with Alain on guard
He entered the hall, where at a great table,
Laden with food and drink, sat the prince
By whose command Rhydian's journey began.
Had it been a trivial bidding, long since
Forgotten in his busy days, or a measured
Charge, seeking to guide a man along his
Allotted path? The young knight stood tall
And spoke to his liege lord, 'If it may please
You sire, I have done your bidding and await
Your orders.' For a moment there was silence,
Then Llewellyn rose and walked towards
Him, laughing with pleasure, 'Your absence
Has been noted, daily I have been asked
When you will arrive.' He looked puzzled,
For who was here that knew, or cared, about
Him. 'Come, sit by me, keep me enthralled
With your adventures, I am bored with old
Tales and need something new to lighten
The long evenings.' 'Firstly I must request
Directions to stabling for my horse, then

Lodgings for my companion, they are tired
And in need of sustenance, I cannot rest
Myself, until they are properly cared for.'
At this reply the prince smiled, 'As my guest
You may keep your horse with mine, your
Companion is welcome here, to join with me.'
Saying to a youth beside him, 'Tegwared
Give our friend assistance, and I foresee
On his return, a night of entertainment.'

Gwen

Tegwared led them to the castell stables
Watching as Rhydian settled horse and hound
For the night, fetching fresh hay and straw
Pouring cool water into the trough, he found
This strange and asked why a knight worked
Thus, for surely that was the squire's duty.
Rhydian laughed, but made no response,
Then, all done, they returned to the lofty
Hall. Llewellyn beckoned to seats along
The dais, pushing a trencher, full of meat
And bread, towards them. Taking a flagon
Of deep red heady wine, he filled a goblet
And handed it to Rhydian, which he quietly
Set aside, taking instead a flagon of water.
As the prince had ordered he began to relate
His journey, a fine tale, told without falter.
Yet he found a reluctance to tell the whole,
No mention was made of the water sprite
With her dark hair and deep, deep, blue eyes.
Nor were his dreams told, afraid they might
Be misunderstood. As his tale came to an end
Some were ready for sleep, others, head
Fuelled by wine were seeking a new sport
Looking for a woman to warm their bed.
They left the hall, promising to return soon
With a lusty wench for Rhydian. He turned
Quite pale, and stood up to leave, begging
Indulgence from his Lord, saying he yearned
For rest after his long day. With a curious
Stare Prince Llewellyn bid him goodnight.
Together with Alain, Rhydian went to the place
Where he felt safe, sleeping until the daylight,

Shining through the stable door, woke them.
The castell was quiet, apart from the villeins
No one was yet astir as early in the morning
Rhydian rode Cadair out. Going fast through lanes
And meadows he reached the river. Stripping
Off his clothes he ran into the water, the cold
Making him draw sharp breaths. He chased
Silver fish, diving down to the reeds, a bold
Otter swam with him, proving to be a better
Hunter by catching his breakfast which he ate
Whilst lying on his back, his black beady eye
Watching warily, ever ready to take flight.
Climbing out onto the bank Rhydian reached
For his clothes, blindly brushing the water
From his face, he felt a shadow fall across
Him. Looking up he saw a face, now softer
In the morning light than when reflected
Through the river. Without feeling shame
In his nakedness he reached out and touched
Her face for the first time, creating a flame
That coursed through his body waking
Senses that had until now lain dormant.
With sudden awareness of time and place
He hastily donned his clothes, the potent
Presence of this young maiden causing him
Some confusion. Together they rode back,
Her arms encircling his waist, her cheek
Resting on his shoulder, her long black
Hair lying across his face. As they reached
The stable Alain ran out, in sheer delight,
Calling loudly 'Rhydian! Gwendydd!'
His joy was without bounds at the sight
Of his two most beloved people, together.

The Challenge

From the dark shadows of the castle walls
A still figure watched as Gwen embraced
Her young brother, noting every move
She made, how her waist was encircled
By the young knight's arm, with her head
Resting on his shoulder. As the sound
Of her voice, with its lilting cadence,
Reached the onlooker, words drowned
By the everyday noises from the castell,
His thoughts grew blacker and hatred
Grew for the newcomer. The girl suddenly
Moved, as if aware of time passing, she fled
Back to the lady tower. Keeping out of sight,
The silent watcher followed her, entering
The main hall to rejoin the Prince's retinue,
There he awaited the return of Rhydian.
When he entered later, Llewellyn greeted
Him with laughter, 'You are an early riser,
I see we will have to give up our feasting
If we wish to catch you. Sit here, by the fire
With me, you intrigue me, not being in the
Usual fashion of a young man, last night
I saw your dislike of our rowdy melee
You left the hall suddenly, in full flight,
Yet you do not have the look of a monk.'
'Sometimes I prefer quieter pastimes,
Yet am not, I trust, a killjoy. I can tell
Tales, sing and play songs, with rhymes
As bawdy as the rest, but also keep my own
Company, with time for much thought.
It is true I withdrew from the lusty games,
But I vowed to refrain from Venus' sport

79

Until my quest is done, I entreat you not
To divert me along my chosen pathway.'
The prince, gazing at the upright figure,
Felt a moment of sadness for the day
When he too, had held such high ideals.
'I will not stand in your way, but trust
That whilst you remain here with me
There will be time, before your quest,
Whatever that may be, takes you further,
Gracing us with your company, fighting
In our tourneys, breaking a few maidens'
Hearts along the way, and then singing
Us to sleep when our bodies are tired.'
Smiling with pleasure at this command
Rhydian turned to Tegwared, 'Will you also
Be at the jousts? There will be much demand
For places I am sure.' A strange look passed
Over his face, and his voice had a sharp ring
To it as he replied – 'I look forward to a bout
Against you, but I must give you fair warning
The tilt is my favourite sport, I am unbeaten.'
He threw his gauntlet down on the floor,
'A challenge match to whet the appetite
You do not yet know, but I have a score
To settle, better to be soon and not delay.'
Quietly Rhydian picked up the gauntlet
'I accept, but have the right to know why
You have challenged me, you need not fret
I will meet you, but I do not fight without
Reason.' The answer came in tones so low
Only the two could hear it, 'The lady Gwen
Is my betrothed, I will land the fatal blow
That will lay waste your pathetic hopes.'

Gwen's Answer

Rhydian watched the hunting party depart
Seeking game to replenish the larders,
Tegwared leading the riders out of the gate.
No word had passed between them since
The challenge, with the gauntlet thrown
Down. Leaving a confused and sorrowful
Young man behind, feeling lost and alone
In this strange place. Turning towards
The stable he looked up at the ramparts,
To the lady tower, in his imagination seeing
The slim figure of Gwen, wishing his heart's
Desire was beside him now. For if she was
Truly betrothed, he need abide by the Knight's
Code of Conduct, either claiming her through
Battle or he must forever relinquish his rights.
As he brushed Cadair, the steady rhythmic
Physical action calmed his heated mind.
From the doorway he heard a quiet voice
Speaking softly to him, words that entwined
His very soul. With a deep intake of breath
He took her in his arms, tears running freely
Down his cheeks, he buried his face in her hair.
With all the gentleness of a mother, not fully
Understanding his pain, she soothed it away
Until he regained full command of his senses.
With her arms around him they sat on sweet
Smelling hay, Cyfaill's head resting on Gwen's
Kirtle. Rhydian retold the day's encounter with
Tegwared, fearful of her reply. As he spoke
Anger rose in her, till she could not contain it,
An edge to her voice as she replied 'I revoke

That, I am not his betrothed, never have nor
Ever will be. He has lusted after me since
I first arrived. He often comes, unbidden,
To the solar room, thinking, as the Prince
Is his father, that all will fall at his feet.
The Princess Joan will have no truck
With him. His noble sire views him kindly
Favouring him highly above others, luck
Seems to flow in his blood, he has a ready
Wit, good looks and is an accomplished
Knight, but I cannot like him, he can be
Cruel, in ways I do not care for, I tread
Very carefully in my dealings with him.'
They talked again after a few minutes
Of reflection. Gwen telling how she had
Often watched Rhydian as a boy, in visits
To his home by the power of sight, seeing
Him at play, how sad she was when he left
Home, and her happiness when he returned.
'I noted your care for the frail and how deft
You were with sick creatures, you were not
Like the others, never wantonly unkind.
I have loved you well for most of my life,
You are the other half of my soul, I find
That without you I am nothing, an empty
Vessel, with no guiding star to follow.'
For a long while they talked in the peace
Of the stable forgetting what the morrow
Might bring, until Alain found them with
The orders to return, one to her duties
The other to entertain his liege's court.
Their idyll past for now, with more stories
Yet to be told, they obeyed the summons.

The Betrothal

That morn Rhydian spoke to the Prince
Professing his love for Gwen and hers
For him. The full story he did not tell,
Nor was it asked of him, in the hours
They spent in each others company
A respect grew between the hardened
Leader of men and the idealistic youth.
'Rest easy, I will speak to my ardent
Son, in my court no maid should fear
For her honour, nor to be forced into
Unwelcome alliances. The Lady Gwen,
As my ward, has my protection and due
Regard should be given to her wishes.'
With a lightened spirit Rhydian sought
His beloved, finding her with the ladies
Attending to the Princess Joan. A taut
Look crossed her face as she saw him
Leaving the great hall, turning to joy
As he smiled at her. He spoke boldly
To the company, 'You see here a boy,
His heart pierced by Cupid's arrows,
Who craves of you a short time, a few
Moments with the Lady Gwendydd.'
Amid much laughter they withdrew
From the room. There, sitting inside
The private chapel they plighted their
Troth. Rhydian, taking Emrys's ring,
Threaded it on a leather thong, to wear
Around her neck. 'I cannot promise
You any riches, for the road that I tread
May be rough, I am going I know not

Where. But I know that without you I dread
The days ahead. You are my mirrored
Half, yet I do not ask you to face these
Dangers with me, only to be my haven
When I am in need. If it should please
You to share my journey we will walk
Together, equal partners in all we do.'
Holding Emrys's ring in her hands,
Feeling its warmth, she replied 'If you
Are by my side, I am afraid of nothing.'
As he kissed her the door opened wide
And Alain rushed in, unable to contain
His pleasure, 'I could no longer bide
My time and wait, you have been ages.'
Gwen laughed, saying 'You take not
Just me, but my little brother as well,
Take fair warning, for I almost forgot
That he will give us no peace, wanting
Forever to be part of our adventures.'
Rhydian put both his arms around the pair
'Remember you must also take my horse
And hound – and her pups, soon to arrive!'
With this they returned to the hall their
Happiness visible to all who saw them.
But so quickly hope can give way to fear,
As the sound of hooves clattering over
The cobbled yard heralding the return
Of the hunting party. Tegwared halted
His sweating mount in front of Rhydian.
Then, without a word, he turned away.

The Day Arrives

Gwen returned, troubled, to her bower,
Watching as Rhydian slowly made his way
To the hall where Tegwared and his cronies
Still full of the chase, were holding sway.
At his entrance the voices became quiet
All eyes were upon him, waiting for events
To unfold. Holding a straight course past
The party Rhydian walked up to the Prince,
Taking a seat next to him at the high table
Amidst much welcome. The talk soon came
Round to the tourney, Llewellyn and his sons
Led their own teams whose valour and fame
Were legend across the kingdoms. 'A place
Must be found for you.' The hint of a smile
Touched his lips. 'I believe you would be
Happier in my team than in my son's. The trial
Of strength between us is not taken lightly
So practise hard to ensure I do not lose.'
The favour shown to Rhydian by the Prince
Was well marked, causing some to choose
Him as a friend, others to harbour ill will
And resentment against this newcomer.
Rhydian kept his distance from all others,
Preferring his own company, the summer
Evenings bringing untold joy with Gwen.
An older knight, Sir Bedwyn, befriended
Him, giving advice in the rules of jousting,
He also brought him news of Tegwared,
Whose venomous tongue had spread
Unfounded tales, creating a figure of hate.
The day of the tourney dawned amid
Much bustle and excitement, with late

Arrivals camping outside the castle walls.
For the first time since he was knighted
Rhydian wore his regalia with its specially
Designed blazon, donned over borrowed
Armour. Whilst Alain prepared Cadair,
Rhydian, kneeling in front of his sword,
Prayed silently for courage, for he knew
That he faced an opponent who abhorred
Him, and would seek to bring humiliation
To the man who had thwarted his desire
For the lady Gwendydd. Llewellyn had set
The rules of combat, which would require
A steady hand, clear head and brave heart.
The *mêlée a pied* was drawing to its close
As Rhydian left the stable, seeking the tree
Where his shield hung. Fear suddenly rose
Inside him, he began to shake and doubt
Himself. Looking into the crowds his eyes
Searching among the people, seeking for
A familiar face, then he saw him, the wise
Old man of his dreams, Emrys. It seemed
As if time stood still, no sound was heard
Except inside his head, the sound of a crwth
Playing such sweet music. Without a word
Passing between them, his courage returned.

The Joust

Before mounting Cadair he spoke
Gently to him 'We have had many
Adventures, much sport together
Now I place my trust in you, carry
Me boldly, without fear, be sure
Footed and steadfast, together
We will be the victors.' Leading
Him to the nearby block, eager
To start the fray, he rode onto
The field with his lance held high.
The Heralds called for the knights
To make ready. With a mighty cry
The two great horses thundered
Towards each other. The lance's aim
Was true and each found its target.
Turning the horses around they came
Back for the second tilt. Once more
The match was even, yet it seemed
As if Tegwared's anger was rising, for
In this favourite sport, he was deemed
To be the champion. The third and final
Run began, the heavy lance unbalancing
The lighter Rhydian, Tegwared struck
Him full on his shield, Rhydian, keeping
A straight arm, also made hard contact.
Cadair did not waver, enabling his rider
To stay upright. Tired, the other horse,
Stumbled, and with no time to recover
Tegwared tumbled to the ground.
In fury he unsheathed his sword and ran
To Rhydian. 'We have not finished, I have
The right of combat, fight me like a man

Hand to hand.' With his blade he slashed
Out wildly, cutting Cadair's leg till it bled,
Rhydian threw off his helm, dismounting.
The two fought savagely, their feet slid
On the trampled grass as they forgot
The joust, that this was but a game.
With the blood pounding in both their
Veins they battled on, trying to maim
The other in defeat. One went down,
The other closed in for the final thrust.
Their eyes met, death facing the loser,
The sword descended hard, the dust
Rising as it fell harmlessly to the floor.
Rhydian turned and with scalding tears
Flowing down his cheeks walked back
To Cadair, not hearing the crowds jeers,
Branding him a coward at the final point.

After The Joust

In the quiet coolness of the stable
As he tended to Cadair's injured fetlock
Rhydian gathered his troubled thoughts.
Feeling a deep shame he tried to block
The jeers of the crowd from his mind.
He saw the strickened look on the face
Of his opponent as he lay on the floor
How all anger had left him, in its place
The desire to weep at the stupidity of man.
A low voice called, full of love and pride,
Before turning to meet her, Rhydian drew
Himself up straight, yet unable to hide
His greatest fear, that of rejection from
Those he cared for most. Gwen moved
Towards him, taking him in her arms
They stood together in silence, soothed
By the closeness of their warm bodies,
With no need for words to pass between
Them. Into this peace came the old knight
Bedwyn, 'This should have been foreseen
I saw you had the gift of grace in your soul.
Be not shamed, you are still a true warrior,
Forged from a different metal to others here.
My Lord Llewellyn sent me here as courier,
Bidding me to bring you to him, he desires
To speak with you.' 'I cannot leave my
Destrier untended, tell my lord I will come
When my squire returns.' Giving this reply
Rhydian returned to the care of his horse.
The older man, sitting down in the straw,
Looked at the young man with respect
For his bravery, to put an animal before

The ruler of the land, to risk his wrath.
'I will wait here, with you and your lady,
It is many years since I have met your equal.'
The door burst open, causing Gwen to cry
With alarm as Alain struggled in, carrying
Cyfaill in his arms, he was covered in blood,
Sweat ran from his brow, as he placed her
On the ground. He gently wiped the mud
From her body as she took deep breaths
Between whimpers of pain. 'She came
To my aid when I was fighting Tegwared's
Friends, I am sorry, I must take the blame,
They kicked her, then ran away, laughing
At the pain inflicted. She could not stand,
So I carried her back here.' Rhydian knelt
By the hound, her tongue licked his hand
As he talked softly to her, stroking her
Body gently. 'I believe she will whelp
Within the hour, brought on too early
By the blows received, she needs help,
But I have no knowledge of these matters.'
The anguish in his voice brought Bedwyn
To his side. 'She will be well, being young
And strong, but not so the pups lying within.
We must keep them warm and dry when
They are born, mayhap they will not draw
Breath without our aid, I will show you
What to do if needed, she just needs more
Time, your presence will be her comfort
And reassurance.' Filling it with water,
Rhydian took Emrys' stone cup, from which
She drank, as her breathing grew quieter
She drifted into a peaceful, healing sleep.

The Whelping

Inside the stable it was still, only the sound
Of breathing to be heard, as all within slept.
The hound began to stir, waking the young
Knight who lay beside her. Slowly he crept
To Bedwyn, asking for advice and guidance.
They watched over Cyfaill as she struggled
To give birth, a large pup began to appear
Black head first, then a wet body emerged.
Taking a large handful of straw Bedwyn
Began to rub the lifeless cenawon, blowing
Gently into his nose, suddenly it sneezed
And taking a breath began whimpering.
Trembling with excitement Rhydian laid it
Beside Cyfaill. Gwen and Alain, now awake,
Danced with joy as yet another pup began
To arrive. But there was also heartache
As one small body did not draw breath.
The door opened and a tall figure entered
Unnoticed. At first he was angry, but this
Soon changed as looking on, he observed
The small group, so intent in their work.
Alain was the first to see him, in surprise
His tiny charge nearly slipped from his hands.
The Prince taking it from him hushed the cries
Then placed it down on the straw bed beside
Cyfaill, who for one last time tried to deliver
Her biggest pup. Seeming to lack the strength
For this final effort, she started to shiver.
The tears in Rhydian's eyes blocked out the face
Of the large man who knelt down beside him,
All he knew was that a pair of knowing hands
Gently eased the cenawon's trapped limb

And with a rush the last of the litter arrived.
It was a few minutes before the realisation
Of who their visitor was dawned on Rhydian.
He stood before Llewellyn with a sensation
Of deep foreboding, for ignoring a summons
Was serious, yet felt no need to explain his lack
Of attention. There before him Llewellyn saw
Bravery such as made saints, but that track
Would not be journeyed down by this youth.
Time stood still as man and boy took measure
Of one another until Llewellyn began to laugh,
'By my troth, I take the greatest pleasure
In being taught a lesson in humility by my
Youngest knight, who reminds me that a lowly
Hound is as important in the eyes of our Lord
As I am. Gwen, I do not believe he is so holy
That I can leave you here with him all night
Return to my lady wife, Sir Rhydian you will
Be at the Hall in the morning, do not fail me
This time, twice would be too many, until
Then I bid you farewell, come Gwendydd.'
Without a backward glance he left, followed
By Gwen and Bedwyn, leaving Rhydian and Alain
With their thoughts, for the morn may not bode
Well if Tegwared should speak first to his sire.

Dismissal

All night long Rhydian kept vigil over Cyfaill and her litter.
Four pups she nursed, one small body sadly buried under
An oak tree in the pleasaunce. He had found great peace
In watching the new lives as they sought to find their place.
Later, walking towards the hall, he wondered what the future
Would bring. A knight's life may not be the path to travel, sure
In the knowledge that his lord had no need for one who failed
To carry through the final blows. He remembered the troubled
Look his mother had given him as she gave him her farewell
Kiss and blessing, had she known her son would be unable to
    kill?
The hall was empty except for the Prince seated at the high
    table,
He beckoned to Rhydian. 'Have no fears, I wish to relate an
    old tale
About a man and his dog, how the man had acted in haste,
    not
Looking for the truth first – A hunter laid his baby son in its
    cot,
Leaving his hound to guard him from the wolves still roaming
The hills. On his return he found the dog, with mouth
    foaming
And bloody. The baby's cradle was empty, believing the hound
Had harmed his son, he killed the dog without a thought. A
    sound
From behind the settle led him to find the truth, his young son
    lay
Unharmed beside the body of a wolf. Had that man learnt to
    stay
His anger and reflect, then a noble life would not have been
    taken.

93

Sir Rhydian, I was that man. Do not believe that I have
   forsaken
You when I say you must leave my court, but others here have
   yet
To grow in understanding, putting your life in peril. I am beset
By people of little vision, who will not see in you the courage
It takes to be different in thought and deed. You have a lineage
To be proud of – a father of integrity, a mother whose
   compassion
Is greatly known – yet you cannot remain with me, I must
   harden
My heart – much though I desire that you remain here at
   court.
I have kept the peace in my lands for many long years, hard
   fought
By a show of strength, your ways would cause my enemies to
   ask
Questions about my leadership. The time will come when my
   task
Is done, but not yet, my sons have not learnt the skills they
   require.
You must leave before Tegwared awakes.' Rhydian replied
   'Sire,
I will leave in my own time I shall not flee like a thief in the
   night.'
'If not for yourself, for Gwen, I cannot keep her ever in my
   sight
She will not be safe if you are there to remind my vengeful
   son
Of his humiliation.' Rhydian considered this, 'I must be
   certain
Of my way, with but an hour's grace, you will have my
   answer"

Llewellyn could only nod his assent, the sorrow he felt was
  greater
Than he could bear, watching the man he would have been
  proud
To call son walk away from him, to face the world, unbowed.

Leaving Court

Leaving the hall Rhydian found Gwen waiting for him,
Eager to hear his news. In measured tones he told
How he had but an hour to decide if he would do
As the Prince commanded. Fear turned Gwen cold
At the thought of losing him, he was her life blood
Without which she would surely die. He knew time
Was short before Tegwared awoke. Gwen smiled
'He will sleep late today, the sun had begun its climb
In the sky before he retired to bed, and the Lady Joan
Slipped a draught in his wine last night, no love is lost
Between those two, and she has a weakness for me.'
Gwen picked up a bundle neatly wrapped and tossed
It in a corner 'I have the few belongings that I desire
To take from here, I have money too for our journey.
When we plighted our troth you said we would find
Our pathway together, I keep my word, you will see
I am my mother's daughter!' As a great weight lifted
From Rhydian's shoulders excitement began to grow
Inside him, he began to plan their leaving, suddenly
The joy left him. 'I cannot leave Cyfaill behind, yet how
Can I take her too?' Laughing Gwen took him inside
The saddle room, pointing to two woven panniers.
'Bronn is strong, she can easily carry our belongings,
Alain and Cyfaill's pups, Cadair will willingly carry us.'
Rhyd gave his lady a long hard look of admiration
He may have the dreams, but the power to take
Them through to reality was hers. 'I will ask Alain
If he wishes to come with us, or stay here and make
His future at Llewllyn's court, where he would be well
Received.' Whilst Gwen returned to the Lady Joan
Rhydian sought out Alain, finding him curled up asleep
Next to Cyfaill, her head on his lap and the tiny roan

Bitch pup nestling in his hand. When Rhydian asked
The question Alain grew angry, 'What manner of man
Do you think I am? I would lay down my life to save
Yours. You insult me by even thinking I could remain
Here.' These words brought colour to Rhydian's face.
'Forgive me, I did not intend to hurt you, but no one
Should travel with me except of their own free will.
I will be honoured for you to join us. Gwen had begun
To plan our going last night, before I knew the need
Was there. She is a wise woman.' Alain gave a shout
Of laughter, 'Be warned, she will cozen you with soft
Words, but rule you with an iron fist, be in no doubt,
For I suffered much when she had me in her charge.'
Rhydian gently ran his hand down Cadair's leg, feeling
For heat, aware that there was no time for the wound
To heal. Alain started to make ready for their leaving
Whilst Rhydian sought out Llewellyn in the Castell keep
To bid him farewell. 'You have much that I envy, loyal
Friends, a lady worthy of your love and a pure spirit
As yet untarnished. Were I younger, without my royal
Duties I would have liked to join you on your quest.
But I have chosen my path, bringing its own reward,
I trust my name will be remembered for many years
After I have left this mortal world.' Taking his sword
He kissed the hilt, then with a sigh, dismissed Rhydian.
No one watched as their party left the Castell, except
For two old men. Bedwyn stood waiting by the gate
For them to pass through, 'Godspeed, I have kept
Guard, the young knights are still sleeping soundly,
You will be long gone when they awake. I do not say
Goodbye, but farewell for I know that we will meet
Yet one more time.' Then he looked across the valley
To where another pair of keen old eyes was watching
The strangely touching group as they started another
Step of the journey. The big horse proudly bore his Lady,

Whilst the steady Bronn carefully carried the mother
And her pups, bound to each other by their friendship.

Part Four

The
Quest

Cadair Idris

Climbing steadily they left the castell far below,
Not stopping until a fair distance lay between
Them and Tegwared. The three peaks of Cadair
Idris rising above, beckoning them to unseen
Places, with the promise of new adventures
Along the way. Their companionable silence
Was broken only by the wind blowing over
The grass, the birds signalling their presence
In song and by the puppies' occasional cries
Lying warm and snug in the large panniers
Slung across Bronn's broad back. Their pace
Was slower than Rhydian wanted, but fears
For Cadair's wound and with Cyfaill not yet
Recovered from her whelping, he was forced
To curb his desire to reach the safety of high
Ground. Stopping by a stream that coursed
Its way down the valley, with good grazing
And shelter from the mountains stony walls
They made camp. Later, sitting by the fire
Rhydian began to speak. 'The mountain calls
To me, I once had a dream which I now must
Follow. Alain, I trust you to care for my lady
Till I return.' Gwen looked troubled as he spoke
'You intend to spend the night alone on the chilly
Mountain, men have lost their wits after a night
On Cadair Idris.' Rhydian smiled at her, 'A vigil
You may keep, watch out for me by a blue lake,
Where I saw, with the eyes of a hawk, a damsel
Walk into its water with a man. I will await their
Return, I have great need of speech with them.'
Gwen watched him run swiftly up the steep track
Through eyes drenched with tears, unable to stem

Them as they ran freely down her cold cheeks,
Until he disappeared from sight. With a deep sigh
She went to the stream and by taking large stones
Created a small pool of clear water, then sitting by
Its edge, and in the way of all women, she waited.
The sun had just dropped behind the mountain
As Rhydian reached the lake, casting long shadows
Across the surface, changing its colours to green
And black, from blue and gold. Suddenly a wind
Springs up, with white waves dancing to the shores
Edge. Music starts to play, reverberating around
The mountain sides, growing louder until it roars
With intensity. All around rocks begin to change
Shape, mythical creatures let loose from captivity.
Rhydian concentrated his mind, bringing sweet
Thoughts to banish his fear, with Gwen's lovely
Face held in his heart he walked calmly towards
The lake. The waves parted, with a path leading
Down towards a cave, where stood a slender figure
Beckoning Rhydian to enter. He hesitated, fearing
To descend into the watery realm, then, with courage
Returned, he followed her through the cave's portal.
Here light was soft, music gentle, a feeling of peace
Surrounded him, time ceased, and he felt immortal.
As his eyes began to close, sleep tried to claim him.
A voice was calling to him, urgent, growing louder
Bringing him back from the brink of surrendering
Himself to this other world. He looked in wonder
At the kingdom under the lake, peopled by maidens
Of beauty such as he had never seen before, singing
That almost hurt the senses with the purity of tone.
There was but one man, with long grey flowing
Hair and beard, standing alone in the cave's centre.
He smiled at the visitor. 'I knew you would return
To find us, I knew the Hawk that circled above us

Carried your spirit within. Come, you will learn
Much about your journey, there are choices yet
To make, you need to understand where and why
Others have failed, for you are not the first knight
To set out on this quest, but I believe that your high
Ideals will guide you to be the one who will succeed.'
For many hours Emrys talked and the young knight
Listened to tales of myths and legends of long ago,
The world around them changed, pale grew the light,
As the colours dimmed to grey, the figures became
Mere shadows, floating on a misty sea. All warmth
Left their bodies until it seemed they would sink
Into despair, yet there was still hidden strength
To be found, deep inside him a flame flickered
And grew, until he was bathed in a shimmering
Light that lit the way ahead, guiding him out
Of the watery cave to the shore above, fading
In the glow of the moon. He fell to the ground
With a weariness he had never known before
And sank into a dreamless sleep, from which
Only the light of the rising sun could restore
His senses to consider all he had seen that night.

Caledfwlch

The sleeping Rhydian stirred as the warm sun
Rose over the mountain peaks, bringing life
Back into his still body, as he began to waken
The memories of last night filled his head.
Stretching cramped limbs his hand touched
Something hard and cold. Rays of light shone
As flashes of red fire leapt out from its faded
Linen cloth. Carefully he unwrapped the cover
Revealing the most beautiful sword ever made,
Its hilt covered in brilliant gems, garnets, rubies
And emeralds. He ran his hand down the blade
So smooth and cold to his touch, yet as he held
It in his hand it felt light as he made sweeping
Strokes in the air. 'That sword was reputedly
Forged by the Elf smith Gofannon, for a king
Of great renown. It is called Caledfwlch.'
Looking at the speaker, he took a pace forward
'Sir Bedwyn, do you follow me? Your presence
Is strange. Tell me, whence comes this sword?'
'The Gwragedd Annwn brought me here to you,
I do not doubt that they also laid the sword down
Beside you as you slept. It has not been seen for
Many years, hidden from man, whilst its renown
Spread far and wide.' Rhydian's mind was troubled
'It is a heavy burden for me to carry, by what reason
Have I been given this charge, for I am not worthy?'
The old knight smiled wryly, 'You have proven
Yourself worthier than others who held that sword,
You can look at its beauty without the desire to own,
This is why you have been chosen to return it and
Its scabbard to the rightful lord, in a place unknown
To but a few, I am one.' Rhydian was thoughtful

'I have seen such a place in my dreams, I believe
That is where I must go.' Quietly picking up
The sword, he turned to bid Sir Bedwyn leave.

Explanations

The sun's shadows had grown long
When Alain, keeping his watch by
The camp, greeted Rhydian's return.
'I had been told that you were nigh,
Your lady, my sister Gwen, sleeps
Now, I beg you leave her to rest.
Since your departure she kept vigil
Not moving from this stream lest
She lost you from her sight, twice
I heard her call out, reaching down
Into the pool as if seeking to hold
Fast to I know not what. This dawn
She smiled, said you were returning
To us, then, Cyfaill beside her, she fell
Asleep.' These words caused him to
Ponder, for twice, when under the spell
Woven in the watery cave, an extra
Strength had come to him, to fight
The malaise which overcame him there.
The rays from the setting sun cast light
Over the sleeping figures, bathing them
In a golden haze, creating such beauty
That it filled his heart with unbearable
Pain. As he watched they stirred, drowsy
With heavy slumber, in that uncertain
World 'twixt sleep and waking, not sure
Of what their eyes tell them. With a cry
Of joy Gwen leapt up, as tears of pure
Happiness ran freely down her face
They embraced. 'I thought you were
Leaving me, I called to you, sending
My love, but the water grew colder

And I could feel you floating away
To a distant place where I could not
Follow. Twice I lived your despair
I held your love closely as I fought
To bring you once more to our world.
As dawn broke this morn on the shore
Of a distant lake I saw you. Now you
Are returned, I am content. I implore
You not to leave me again, but to take
Me with you, to share in any danger
Is far better than be left unknowing
Of your fate.' With a touch so tender
He traced the salty channels on her
Cheeks. 'You gave me the strength
To resist the powers of the Annwn,
Though we travel across the length
Of our land, we will do it together, for
All time. But enough I have much to tell
You, Alain too.' There in the grassy glade
He told his story, as the dark of night fell
And the firelight grew brighter, he took out
Caledfwlch from its cover, the gleaming
Hilt shone, the stones reflecting the colours
Of the flames, its blade seemed to be a living
Being, quivering, yet icy cold to the touch.
Gwen stared at it in awe, stretching her hand
Out towards it, then withdrawing it in fear.
'This could ruin men's lives, it will demand
From all who wear it their very soul. Made
Not with love, but with the desire to rule.
The desire to own it will make even just
And peaceful men become mad and cruel.'
He then related the charge put on him
To seek its scabbard and return them both
To their rightful Lord. 'I wondered long

On why I was chosen, but if you are loth
For me to continue, I will forsake my quest,
Return to my father's land. Yet there must be
A reason why it has been given to my charge.'
Alain then spoke, 'The reason is that you see
It, can admire its beauty, yet do not covet it.
You have not taken another's life, following
Your own path without any desire for gain.
For only such a person could safely bring
The two parts together, then once united
Not use them to further their own cause.'
Gwen smiled at her brother, for his wisdom
Far exceeded his years. 'You give me pause
For thought. I can, with your help, at least
Attempt to finish this quest, though where
Or how I will find the scabbard, I know not.'
Gwen laughed, 'Be not concerned, for I fear
It will find you, no matter where you may be.'
With a rueful laugh, Rhydian thought so too,
For his adventures had befallen him, unasked.
'Then let us sleep now, for we must continue
Northwards. The mountain paths are narrow,
And steep, For a destrier this is a hard journey,
Cadair is not built to traverse such mountains
Bronn, who was born on the hills, has the agility
Needed to guide us over the ancient ways.'

A Doleful Place

For a few days they rested in the glade,
Bathing Cadair's leg in the streams clear
Water, watching the pups as they grew
Stronger, eyes open, looking without fear
At their new world, safe in Cyfaill's keep.
In this peaceful place they drew closer
Together, with no need for other company.
Laughter and tales shared, taking longer
In the telling as the moon cast its silver
Light bathing all in a shimmering glow.
Soon the time came to leave, once more
To resume their journey, leaving the low
Ground, taking the high pass northwards.
Steady Bronn leading the way, pups snug
On her back, watched over by Alain as
He walked beside her, with Aldan's rug
Keeping them warm. Cadair followed
Finding the narrow pony paths hard
To traverse. Rhydian watched his lady
As she climbed with ease, she laughed
At him, 'You forget, I was born in the hills,
Alain and I ran like wild animals all day
Long, have no doubt, I can outpace you.'
That night their bed was hard as they lay
On granite rocks, tired from their journey
They slept together with the innocence
Of children, no dreams to disturb them.
Woken by the morning sun to a sense
Of joy at just being alive, they continued
Onwards, taking the mountain ridgeway
Until they started to descend, the path
Finally reaching the deep river valley

Where verdant meadows and deep lakes
Beckoned, beauty that enticed them to tarry.
In such an idyllic place their pace slowed,
Stopping by the lake shores, in no hurry
To reach the small town by the fording
Point of the river. 'I want to savour
These moments, good memories that
I can lock inside my mind, to recover
Them when I am sad or afraid, a shield
To protect my soul in times of darkness.'
Gwen stood close by him, afraid to look
Into the water that ran beside her, least
She saw visions of the dangers that would
Surely lie ahead. They stopped for the night
Outside the town, at the edge of a wide flat
Meadow in the shelter of trees, out of sight
Of the houses. As he slept, Rhydian dreamt
Once more he could see and hear strangers,
Yet these people spoke a language he knew,
The tongue of his birth. He felt many dangers
Abounded here, much anger and sadness too.
These people were weary, in body and spirit.
Soldiers stood guard, cruel whips cracked
In their hands. All hope had gone, no fight
Was left within them. He tried to understand
The words around him, but only one phrase
Reached him. 'To enslave another human
Is to take away his humanity, yet I can raise
My eyes to the hills and soar free as a bird
In my imagination.' Spoken by an old man,
Searching through the murky light, looking
Until he found the dream held Rhydian.
Then satisfied, the old man lay down to sleep.
When he awoke the air was full of mist
And low cloud, water droplets hung on all.

110

Quickly he stirred the others, and in haste
They made ready to move. 'I do not wish
To stay here, we will stop instead at Cymer
Abbey, I have a letter of introduction from
Brother Thomas, I believe we will be safer
There than if we stay in this doleful place.'

Cymer Abbey

The mist hung low as they forded the river
Whilst the grey town still quietly slept.
Making haste they took the wide river path
Towards Cymer Abbey. The sunrise crept
Over the valley, sending warmth to dispel
The chilly air. It was but a short journey
To Cymer where, lying under the watchful
Eye of a ruined, hilltop castle, the Abbey
Began to stir. Sheep grazing with cattle
In the water meadows, black and white
Wandering peacefully in the morning sun
Lazily looking as Rhydian came into sight.
Their arrival was also noted by a brother,
A strong swarthy man whose sombre face
Lit with delight when he saw the travellers.
Hurrying to greet them in a loving embrace.
'I knew you would be here soon, Emrys
Sent word, come and break fast with me.'
Leading the way into the cobbled yard
Ythel opened the stable doors, 'You see,
I had all prepared, the ci bach will be safe
Here, your hound can rest, she looks tired
And has not much flesh on her.' Rhydian
Laughed with pleasure, then he replied
'Cyfaill will transfer her allegiance to you
I fear, she has been sorely tried these last
Few weeks.' Later, when all the brothers
Left and were about their work, the repast
Finished, stories were told. Ythel's tale
Was simple, the Abbey at Cymer had need
Of his skills and strength, health restored

He left behind Ystrad Fflur and journeyed
To this place, where, full in the Lord's glory
Laboured to build the abbey church, caring
For the animals and finding a peace, such
As he had never known, in this small loving
Community. Listening to the contentment
In this Cornish wrestler's voice, Rhydian
Thought of the mysterious ways of the Lord.
Desiring time and space for contemplation
He left the others and followed the old track
To the castell ruins sitting a'top of the hill.
Wandering amongst the scorched timbers,
His mind heard the cries of anguish, shrill
Voices and fleeing footsteps as the flames
Surrounded them, with no choice but to stay
And perish, or to fight and die in battle.
Now beauty was all around, the grim play
Finished. Sitting on the cool grass, sleep
And dreams visited him, so real he could
Touch the people who inhabited the land.
A tall Roman, wearing purple on his hood,
Held a young maiden in his arms, gently
Stroking her hair and wiping tears away
From her face. 'Weep not my own Cariad,
I have been granted permission, this day,
By my noble father, to take you as my wife.
He is not pleased, as the son of Macsen
I should be following the campaign trail,
Seeking glory and taking a lady like Elen,
My own mother, as my bride, not a slave
Girl from the mines, even though she has
No compare in beauty or soul in this land.'
As the dreamer looked, he saw in the man's
Face his father's eyes, and in the girl's voice

His melodic lilt, reaching across the years.
As the dream faded it seemed that the love
Of long ago had taken away those fears
Still lingering around the castell mound.

A New Companion

Rhydian, returning to the Abbey grounds,
Watched as Cyfaill's pups played, running
On short wobbly legs, with excited sounds
They explored, whilst keeping close by.
Gwen was sitting on the grass laughing
At their games, the biggest, boldest one,
His coat as black as night, made darting
Attacks at her feet, until suddenly tired
He returned to his mother's side to feed.
As she saw him approach, Gwen gave
A cry of delight, and making all speed
Reached his outstretched arms, a warm
Glow of contentment filling her being.
As he held her close he remembered
The two lovers of his dream, a feeling
That they were smiling down on him,
Sending their blessing across the years.
Gently caressing her hair, Rhydian told
His lady a story, of a slave girl's fears,
And of the Roman noble who loved her.
The evening star rose above the abbey
As Ythel called them to enter within.
'Our fare is plain, but there is plenty
For all, tonight I have an old friend
Staying, he is eager to talk with you.'
In the hall the fire cast long shadows
Its glow lit up the faces of those who
Sat in comradeship, they had no need
For speech, simply sharing their meal
And thoughts. Alone, in a quiet corner,
A man sat, so still, he seemed not real,
As if he was carved of stone, yet there

Was a warmth, a softness, all around
Him, that promised all whom he knew
A safe haven to rest in. Rhydian found
He was drawn towards this man by an
Invisible thread, binding them together
For all time. The man looked up as he
Entered, beckoning 'Ythel, my Brother,
Come to me, I am desirous of speech
With this young man. I have heard tales
Of his chivalry, of his skill with a crwth
That charms all, of a voice that assails
The senses. I wish to meet this paragon
Of virtue to make my own judgement.'
His eyes shone with delight as his words
Caused discomfiture, a flush of brilliant
Red suffusing Rhydian's face, he laughed
Ruefully, and sat beside Ythel's friend.
'My name is Gwyhyr, I have travelled far
And wide over this fair land, now I intend
To cease, just one more place to visit, one
More demon to lay to rest, then I will roam
No more. I go to Dinas Ffaraon, just a few
Days journey away, would you care to come
With me?' He bowed to Gwen, 'If your
Lovely lady will grant me this pleasure.'
Gwen looked into the green of his eyes
Then she replied, 'I have your measure,
And so I give you my lord, guard him well,
As your journeys are drawing to an end,
So his have yet to run their full course.'
'You have wisdom and beauty combined,
To be cherished and protected, yet I see
A courage that lies beneath, where no fear
Will hold you back from your chosen path,
I pledge my life to those that you hold dear.'

116

Goodbye

The two made preparations for their departure
Alain once more had care of Cadair, now Bronn too.
Ythel took charge of Cyfaill and her pups, unsure
If she would fret for her beloved master he sought
Gwyhyr's advice. 'Do not worry, I have spoken
To the hound and she rests easy now. My friend,
I have a fear, the times ahead seem to darken,
Yet I believe this young knight will bring a light
To show us the way, maybe not a glorious flame
But a steady glow that all can approach and feel
Its warmth without fear of burning. Not a name
To live in men's dreams, but a base upon which
The future of our children's children can be built.'
As the morning sun rose over the hills the youth,
Crwth slung over his shoulder, felt a pang of guilt
As he left his lady behind, for he was eager to go
And seek new horizons. 'I give you my promise
That wherever I go, you will be with me, tightly
Held inside my heart. I will return by the next rise
Of the new moon.' Placing a soft kiss on her lips
He waved goodbye, and strode out of the Abbey
Gate. Gwen watched until the two had vanished
From her sight. Then, sitting under the shady tree,
A hound pup held closely, she let her tears flow.

The Next Step

The travellers soon left the Abbey far behind,
A green track led them alongside the rivers edge
Bounded on all sides by steep mountain slopes.
Along one side ran a pale scar, creating a ledge
Wide enough for several men to walk abreast.
As he looked along its length, he saw moving
Shadows, many people walking the dusty road.
Listening intently he could hear voices drifting
On the breeze across the valley. As if pulled by
An invisible hand he left his companion's side
And walked towards the sounds until reaching
A mountain track, he stopped, eyes open wide,
Searching the bare hills. Doubt creeping inside
His mind, had those figures been a distant echo
From a time long past, or a trick of the morning
Light? The way ahead was lit by the sun's glow
As it climbed high in the sky, with a firm step
He followed it, scarce noticing his companion
Walking beside him. They travelled in silence
Each one deep in their own thoughts. Rhydian
Began to sing quietly, strumming the melody
On his crwth, the notes floating on the wind
Until they were caught by the birds of the air
Creating a concert of such vision that a blind
Man could see, music of such sweet intensity
Even the deaf could hear. Gradually his song
Faded away, until it was only in the memory,
Where it would stay hidden till in some long
Time, yet to come it would rise again, there
To bring comfort, awake again the warmth
That crept into ones soul, feeding the belief

THE QUEST

In immortality, giving courage and strength
To journey on. Without a word being passed
The two men, one but a golden-haired youth,
The other who seemed as old as time itself,
Continued down the road, seeking their truth.
That night they made camp by the side of the
Old road and as darkness fell each told a tale,
Rhydian reliving the dream when he became
A Hawk, how it felt to fly over hill and dale
Sharpened senses and the freedom of the air.
Then it was Gwyhyr's turn, struggling to find
The words, as if he was unused to speaking,
He told of knights from olden times, the kind
Of tales that passed away long winter nights
Gradually his voice seemed to change, taking
A new, hypnotic, quality. Slowly as Rhydian's
Eyelids drooped, he slept. An Owl, swooping
On silent wings in the night sky, came to rest
On the tree above them, calling to Gwyhyr
With the understanding of an old friendship.
Man and bird, together as equals, without fear
Using a common language, shared their minds.

The Raven

A large black raven flew ahead of the two men
As they walked the long track, the steady beat
Of its wings stirring the air as it rose high above
The hillside, its distinctive call seeking to greet
The new day. It tumbled and dived as if full of
Joy, it passed over the grass covered stone ruins
The like of others Rhydian had passed before.
He could feel a bleakness here that frightens
Warmth away, yet seemed to beg him to tarry,
Promising wondrous secrets for him to discover.
As he stopped, the raven turned and circled him,
Lower and lower he flew, reaching ever closer
Until his feathers touched Rhydian, urging him
Forward once more, until he was again matching
Gwyhyr stride for stride towards a destination
As yet unknown. Far in the distance, flickering
Reflections of light from water held captive
In a mountain lake created a rhythm, a dance,
That captured the rays from the sun, bending
Them, curling them, then straight as a lance
Spread across the land, colour bursting forth,
Making each step he took lighter, the ground
Smoother. Drawing closer, he could see a house
By the river's edge, with a fishing net around
A small boat. A young woman, catching sight
Of them, called to her children and went inside
Their home, barring the door. They could feel
Frightened eyes watching them, a baby cried
Suddenly, breaking the eerie silence, until just
As quickly it stopped. The two men took rest
By the lakeside, Rhydian looking hopefully

In the still water, praying that he be blessed
With the sight of Gwen's sweet face, but saw
Only his own reflection, which as he looked
Disappeared. A quiet voice spoke to him, yet
He could see no one. The raven scratched
In the fern clad hillside, its glossy black head
Tilted towards him, a beady eye glistened
With all the ancient knowledge of its kind.
The voice came again, and as he listened
Words formed inside his mind, 'Look at me
What see you there?' A long shadow grew
Beside him as the raven rose high into the sky
Watching, it soared, faster and faster it flew,
Turning, until his eyes could follow it no more,
With feather's glowing in the sun's reflected
Rays. One moment they shone with brilliant
Light, burnishing them until they were as red
As sunset, then as quickly becoming a pure
White and for a moment, took another form
Until across the sky, a dragon swooped,
Then gathering speed it vanished. A warm
Wind sprang up, riding it, the raven returned
Landing on the grass, with its shiny black
Eye laughing with delight at the trick played
On the watcher, who, unsure, looked back
Without understanding, but full of wonder.

Tomen y Mur

The two men walked together in easy silence,
With a friendship that belied the short days
Since they had first met, taking the old road
High above the valley floor, following ways
No longer trodden. All the time the raven kept
Them in his sight, circling, watching, calling
With his harsh cry, piercing inside Rhydian's
Mind, filling it with strange sounds, seeming
To create words that he almost understood.
He felt the bird's intelligent gaze upon him,
Mocking him, daring him to a duel of wits.
Suddenly he soared upwards, until a dim
Speck in the blue sky. For a brief moment
Rhydian hardly moved, scarcely drawing
Breath, until, gathering himself together,
He once more followed the track, taking
His place beside Gwyhyr. 'Tell me about
The raven, why does he choose to come
With us? At times, for no known reason,
I have fear of him.' 'I have known some
Of his kind who cannot be trusted, Menw
Is not such a one. He has been a true friend
For many years, with much wisdom learnt
From times long past, you can ever depend
On him to come to your aid when needed.'
They continued onwards, their paces evenly
Matched, they walked to a steady rhythm,
Where the wild moorland could quickly
Change from quiet beauty to a savage
Beast as the rain and wind swept along
The open tracks. A feeling of desolation
Descended upon Rhydian, chasing song

From his heart, the cold reached inside
His soul, slowing his steps till he came
To a standstill. Far away he could see
People gathering, shadows, the same
As before. He could hear a low sound,
The excited hum of anticipation spread
Towards him, gradually he was pulled,
Inexorably, into that crowd, as if led
By an unseen hand until he could move
No more. The crowds parted, revealing
An amphitheatre, where games of war
Were played, with the winner taking
The glory as many a brave man died.
A young girl, heavy with child, tears
Running unchecked ran into the ring,
She knelt beside a soldier all her fears
Held in her being as she gently cradled
Him in her arms. He touched her face
Softly, 'I have loved you above all things,
Hold that deep in your heart and place
Your trust in the Lord, I will find a way
To guide you. My mother, the Lady Elen,
Will care for you and our child.' His gaze
Seemed to rest on Rhydian, though none
Could see him, a smile of contentment lit
His eyes as he gently let go of this life.
The shadows faded away until all had gone,
With only a circle of grass where the strife
Had been and the wind the only sound.

A Perilous Journey

The track led onwards along the high ways,
Across wild heathland with only the hardy
Ponies and sheep to share the solitude.
The land before them dropped suddenly,
Streams gathered pace, cutting sharp
Paths into the land. Far in the distance
The sea sparkled with reflected light
From the sun, whose fiery brilliance
Turned the rivers below into molten
Lava flowing between the wide yellow
Sandbanks, with high tree-covered cliffs
Rising from estuary shores that tower
Upwards to the craggy mountain tops.
Rhydian stood still in silent worship
The beauty taking his breath away,
Gwyhyr beside him, a bond of kinship
Held the two men, a sense of timeless
Knowledge. As the sun sank gradually
Below the horizon, all colour faded
Away, the light becoming a memory
Until only shades of grey remained.
'Tomorrow we will travel those rivers
Using the ebb and flow of the tides
To take us on our journey, to traverse
A dangerous passage, but it will save
Many hours of walking. Let us pray
For a fair wind and a tranquil sea.'
The sun rose in the morn, a fair day
Promised as they made an early start.
The path down by the stream was steep
As it tumbled over rocks, eager to reach
The river and then the sea. The deep

Ravine broadening until it reached the
Shore, where stood an ancient harbour.
Half hidden in a sandy cove, a coracle
Lay, its long oar resting, as if waiting for
Them. Gwrhyr smiled, 'Come my friend,
Be brave, although but a small craft,
The men of Din-Gonwy have made it well
It will carry us with ease, take the aft
Seat, and keep watch for the changing
Currents.' Then taken by the ebbing tide
Between vast sand banks, along deeply
Cut channels twisting from side to side
Passing small hillocks, sometime isles,
With the open sea getting ever closer.
As they rounded the headland a wind
Sprang up, creating waves on the water.
Using all his strength and guile Gwrhyr
Steered a course round the headland,
Making for the river and quiet waters.
As their safe haven seemed at hand
A sudden gust lifted the slender boat
Into the whirling eddies of the sea.
The waves swept Rhydian into the cold
Water away from the Glaslyn estuary
Far from the safety of nearby land.
For all his youthful strength the tide
Had too great a pull, carrying him
Into the mighty ocean. As he prayed
For courage he saw the black raven
Speeding towards him, wings held
Flat against his body the great bird
Dived under the waves, water sprayed
Rhydian's face. Unable to see, he felt
His body being lifted like a feather
Through the water. So fast did they

Travel he could not tell the manner
Of his rescuer, only feel the power
And warmth of the body he rode.
As they reached calmer, sheltered
Water he saw the truth of tales told
By sailors, for he was astride the back
Of a sleek dolphin. 'Menw, my friend,
You are that most magical of beings,
A shape changer, God did indeed send
Me help when I asked for it. I owe you
My life, one day my debt will be repaid.'
Gently he slipped into the sea swimming
For shore, watching as the coracle made
Headway through the sea, impatiently
Waiting to tell of his adventures, yet afraid
His many questions would have no answer.

Menw's Tale

In the wide sheltered estuary, the flowing tide safely carried
The coracle towards the pass where the river Glaslyn sped
Through its rocky gorge to the sea. They took the slim path
    winding
Beside the water as it gathered pace, fed by the streams falling
Down the mountainside. Spray covering them as they traversed
Narrow ledges of overhanging rocks, slipping on moss covered
Boulders they struggled to stay the course. Resting for a while
With beauty all around them, Gwyhyr answered, with a smile,
The faltering questions his young companion asked. 'I will tell
    you
A tale from long ago to bring understanding of our friend
    Menw,
Who dwells in the shadows of time, one of the few who remain
From an ancient race of people in the Western Isle, the
    domain
Of the children of Llyr, whose sorrow held sway for long
    years.
The Eiddlig Gor took sanctuary in the caves, creating many
    fears
With their dark looks and strong magical powers. Much
    mistrust
Abounded. Menw's people were hunted until only the strongest
Shape shifters survived, taking for safety to the water and air,
Keeping their true form hidden from all but a few. But beware
If you bring harm to their kind for they have long memories
And long lives. Many years ago Menw had a young friend,
    boys
Together, both possessing rare gifts, for which they were greatly
Feared. One day his companion was taken by the men of
    mighty

127

Guorthigern, to the high mountains of Eryri, there to be an
    offering
To appease the gods, for the blood of a fatherless boy would
    bring
Strength and firm foundations to his fortress. Taking a raven's
    form
Menw followed, keeping watch o'er his friend, through a great
    storm,
Over wild land, it was a hard flight for one so young, not yet
    grown
Fully into all his powers, during nightfall he rested close by,
    alone
With his fears for what fate awaited them. Before the journey's
    end
His agile mind had devised a plan, which he shared with his
    friend.'
Gwyhyr stopped to draw breath, 'I will tell you no more of
    this tale
Until Dinas Ffaraon, where an ancient task awaits, we must
    not fail.'

The Scabbard

Reaching Bekelert they rested at the small Augustine Priory
Before setting out for Dinas Ffaraon, the end of their journey.
Sitting on top of the rocky hill was a strong square tower
From which flew the standard of Prince Llewellyn, a figure
Stood on the ramparts, watching their approach. The raven
Flew over him, circling high before landing in the bracken
Surrounding the fort, his presence giving Rhydian courage
To face the Prince, then he and Gwyhyr crossed the bridge
Into the courtyard. Here there was but a small hunting party,
A group of men enjoying the game abounding in this lonely
Place. Rhydian was greeted with great pleasure and delight
By Llewellyn, 'My young minstrel, you are indeed a sight
That warms my heart, I have much need of entertainment
Here, with none for company but these men, battle valiant
But without knowledge of music, their only songs bawdy,
Tavern ditties, but tonight I will listen again to the beauty
Of your voice.' Seeing his young guest searching the faces
Of his men, Llewellyn smiled, 'My son Tegwared remains
At Castell y Bere, soothing his hurt pride with another fair
Maiden, I trust your lady is well protected, she did not care
To accompany you here, or is she, methinks, with child?'
Laughing at the blushing youth, 'Or have you not defiled
Her yet, is she still a virgin?' Replying with quiet dignity
Rhydian said 'Until my quest is complete I will not marry
My lady, then with the blessing of my parents and God
We will become as one.' 'It is not my way, though I applaud
Your honour, but enough of this, bring your friend inside
And tell me of your adventures since last we met, hide
Nothing in the telling.' That night they fed well, drinking
Until the early hours, then sank into deep sleep, dreaming
Of home and the families they left behind, of the women

129

Waiting patiently for their return. As sleep came Rhydian
Heard Gwyhyr talking softly, an unknown voice replied,
And somewhere in the distance a tormented soul cried.
In the morning Rhydian awoke, rising before all others,
He walked to the llyn, swimming in its cool clear waters
He felt cleansed in body and mind. The rocky shoreline
Beckoned, enticing him to climb onto a carreg, a fine
Eryr floated above him, riding the thermal air waves.
Behind him tall trees grew thickly, concealing a cave's
Entrance, just visible from his seat, curious, he entered.
A green light lit the inside, showing rough steps hewed
Into the side, leading upwards to the light source, wide
Enough for a youth to climb. His slender frame belied
The strength he possessed, and using this, he climbed
The dark narrow steps, towards the light that shined
Down from the top. Emerging from the shaft he found
Himself in a secluded glade, with no way out, bound
On all sides by sheer, smooth, granite. As he walked
Away from the steps, towards the wall, a bell chimed
From deep inside the hillside. Stretching out his hand
To touch the surface, a great rock slid back. Spanned
Across a chasm was a stone bridge lit by soft candles
Leading to a golden casket, Rhydian entered, prayers
To God filled his mind, asking for the lord's guidance.
The casket opened as he approached, the brilliance
Of the gold contrasted by the plainness of its content
There, lying on a cloth of silk, wrapped in a fragment
Of coarse linen, was an old, brown, leather scabbard.
As Rhydian carefully held this, the casket wavered
And then faded away. With the candle lights dimming
He returned quickly over the bridge, tightly clasping
The scabbard. The egress closed behind as he once
Again climbed the steps to the cave, from whence
He returned to the fort, seeking Gwyhyr eager to tell
Him the tale, sure that his wisdom would explain all.

Concealment

Gwyhyr greeted Rhydian as he entered the main gate,
'I have been watching for you, quickly, it is getting late
And soon all will wake, you must hide your precious
Burden, for its presence here makes me very anxious
For your safety.' Speedily they entered the chamber
Rhydian's belongings were spread out, his leather outer
Jerkin had the silken lining ripped at the seam. Slipping
The scabbard inside, Gwyhyr carefully began stitching
The garment, all the time talking. 'Menw watched your
Adventure this morning, when he heard the bell and saw
The door open, he knew that Myrddyn's treasure casket
Would be found, the enchantment placed would only let
A youth of pure spirit enter. Over time men had sought
In vain to find that entrance, they had bitterly fought
And died in chasing the legend of riches they believed
Lay under this hill. I need more time, events have
    moved
Too fast. Take heed of me, your story is best left untold.'
The early morning sun was rising high, chasing the cold
Air away, as they approached the Prince and his retinue
Preparing for another days hunting. 'Goodbye Menw,
God speed and a safe return.' Gwyhyr's words, softly
Spoken, almost a thought, floating on the wind, free
As the bird they blessed, echoed in Rhydian's mind.
He longed to ask questions, yet for now he must find
Patience. The Prince called to them, 'You must hunt
With us Sir Rhydian, I will provide you with a mount.'
Gwyhyr smiled at the eager face of his young friend,
'Go and enjoy the chase, but take note of this, I intend
To feast well tonight, be sure the twrch does not escape.'
Seeking quiet he climbed the walls, a plan taking shape,
A way for Rhydian to complete the task he had been set.

How difficult that would be, what temptations to be met,
Was still unknown. Over long centuries many others tried,
Valiant men, but without a true purity of spirit, had failed.

The Legend Of The Red Dragon

That evening in the great hall there was much merriment
The twrch was slowly turning on the spit, voices, strident
In their efforts to be heard, vied with each other, telling
Tales of the chase, each story growing, with much vying
Among the knights, of their bravery and the tracking skill
That led them to the prey, until, glorying in the final kill
They returned home, bone weary and ready for the feast.
Rhydian joined in the fun, yet as he looked at the beast
He felt a sadness, but took comfort that it was his keen
Sword thrust that ended the struggle, a swift and clean
End to a worthy opponent. 'Come minstrel boy, bring
Memories of the ladies we left behind, you must sing
For your ale tonight.' The Prince's words were echoed
Around the room, until amid cheers, Rhydian was lifted
Onto a wooden table. Laughing he began to sing, bawdy
Songs, ballads, childhood rhymes that all joined, until he
Could sing no more. The Prince applauded, then called
To Gwyhyr, 'I know of you, that many a tale you have told
To while away the long winter's nights, tell us the legend
Of this place. I know it well, as a child I oft have listened
And many is the hour that I spent searching for dragons.'
'I will gladly re-tell the old tale, there are many versions,
Mine is one not well known, yet methinks it may be nearer
To the truth than others.' His figure seeming to grow taller
As he began to speak, he retold the familiar, ancient tale
Of how a mighty ruler, a fierce fighter in battle, could fail
To build a castle that stood upright. His listeners knowing
Full well the story cheered the red dragon vanquishing
The white Saxon intruder, yet fell silent at the final twist.
For Gwyhyr told a different ending, 'Out of the mist
Emerged the victor, his red scales reflecting the fiery
Tongues of flame he blew at those gathered close by.

The boy, Ambrosius, turned to Guorthigern addressing
Him and his men. *You must leave this place, no building
Will stand here for many years, take the road westwards
To the Llŷn, there you will find a hill, looking outwards
To the sea on all sides. Here will be your new fortress
Where your people can live in safety, but sacred fires
Shall descend until you are consumed and your sons
Will rule a divided realm. My knowledge of the dragons
Is from the past, this is of the future. Your line will pay
Homage to a king, whose name will live till doomsday.*
That night Guorthigern sought out Ambrosius, intending
To slay him, in fear of his prophecies. As he was entering
The bedchamber he heard laughter, the joyous sound
Of children playing. He watched as one turned round
And round, too quickly for Guorthigern's eyes to follow.
The boy changed colour, red, white, green and yellow
Until it seemed there was not just one child, but four.
Suddenly he stopped, and looked towards the door.
Ambrosius called out, *Enter, Come and meet the red
Dragon of Cymru, but be careful, he has not yet fed
With his help we shall be able to foretell your future.*
As he watched, the small unknown boy grew in stature,
Changing shape, growing wings and a long, sinuous, tail,
His red scales glowing with fire. With a frightening wail
The brave warrior king turned and fled from the room.
As the dawn rose on the following day, an air of gloom
Lay around as Guorthigern ordered all his men to leave.
*I will go to the Llŷn, there to build my Caer, I believe
This dinas belongs to Ambrosius, it is now his stronghold.'*
Finishing speaking Gwyhyr sat down, his story now told.

Preparation

That night, when the Prince and all his men lay sleeping,
Rhydian thought deeply on Gwyhyr's tale, wondering
At this new version of an ancient legend. He believed
That last night the Prince had not been the intended
Audience, but that the story had carried a message
For him to hear and understand, a truth from an age
Long past, awaiting the time when all could finally
Be completed, with those restless spirits set free
From their earth bound prison, for now he was sure
Who his travelling companions were. He did not see
Yet why he was chosen, nor how he could complete
This venture. He almost felt angry, that it was not meet
To place such a burden upon him, yet a feeling of great
Pride surged through his body, he rejoiced in his fate
For was he not a knight and had he not wanted to prove
His worthiness? He thought of Gwen, of his deep love
For her, and as sleep took him he held her smile fast
In his heart. Waking renewed, the events of the past
Day fresh in his mind, he sought Gwyhyr. He found
Him on the Dinas walls, searching the sky southbound.
'My good friend what do you seek in the heavens?'
'I look to Menw's return, for you must leave these bastions
Quickly, but I am loth for you to go until all is in place
For the next part of your journey.' Rhydian turned to face
Gwyhyr – 'Are you leaving me? I need your guidance
Now more than ever' 'I say to you, your conscience
Will guide you better than I, for I have lived on this earth
Too long and am weary. A keen and virtuous youth
Will find the right solution to a centuries old problem,
Created by man's desire, with spirits held in thralldom
Until released by a pure soul that is as yet untouched
By greed and selfishness. Fear not, all have not fled

135

From your side, I see Menw approaches, let us greet
Him.' A Raven swooped down, landing at their feet,
His eye held Gwyhyr's, exchanging a silent message.
'We must find the Prince, and ask for safe passage
Out of his lands, now your quest moves to its close.
We will accompany you until those that you chose
Are again at your side, for Menw has safely guided
Your lady over the mountains, which held no dread
For her, she would make a truly worthy knight!'
At this news Rhydian could not contain his delight
He looked for Menw, but he was high in the sky
Speeding back to his charges, to bring them safely
To the Bekelert Priory, there to wait for Rhydian
Before they began their final trek, united again.

Part Five
To
The Llŷn

Leaving Court

The two companions made ready for their departure
Before seeking out the prince, Rhydian felt no wiser
About their next step, nor could understand the urgency
For the hurried leave. 'My friend, you fear for me
Yet do not tell me why, I am not a coward, unable
To face dangers, I must know what manner of battle
Awaits me so that I may prepare.' Gwyhyr thought,
'You have the right to know for why it is sought.
Give me your dagger, I will show you the powerful
Treasure you carry and then you will be mindful
Of its danger.' Taking the blade he cut deeply
Into Rhydian's arm, startled at this seemingly
Wanton attack he drew back, unsure, his trust
Faltering. 'Look at the wound Rhydian, you must
Take note, then hold your silence, many would
Kill you if it was known Caledfwlch's scabbard
Had been found. You need to take the two parts
To a place of safety, holy ground where hearts
Are pure and desire for worldly power absent.'
From the cut, he saw no blood, whilst a pleasant
Warmth ran up his arm, and as he looked in awe
The skin healed, leaving no scar, no sign to show
Where the knife had been. 'As long as you wear
This coat with its hidden burden, you will not fear
Any blade. Without it, you are once more alone.'
For one moment Rhydian felt the desire to own
The sword and scabbard for himself, for surely
He could conquer all others, become the mighty
Knight of his dreams, he would seek and find the grail.
But the knowledge came that to him, a mere mortal,
Such power was too great, the temptation too high

Its possession would destroy the soul, so with a sigh
He took off the jacket, turning away from such glory.
'We shall now depart from here, you weave a story
Of enchantment where reality and fable entwine.'
Carrying all belongings they left to seek Llewelyn,
As they passed, a figure emerged from the shadow,
Following them into the Dinas keep. His pale, sallow,
Features twisting with an unholy smile, he seated
Himself amidst the prince's men as they gathered
Together before the days hunting. Gwyhyr strode
Towards the high table, his long cloak billowed
Out behind him, as they approached men gave
Way, granting them access 'My Lord, we crave
Your permission to continue on our journey west.
We fain to leave your company and so request
Your blessing as we leave, no longer to remain,
To grant us safe passage across your domain.'
After a long thoughtful silence the Prince replied,
'You have my leave, to all men I say woe betide
Any who harms you or yours whilst on the land
I rule. I do not hold sway in the Llŷn, my hand
Cannot protect you there. Before you leave
I have need of talk with you, in truth I believe
You are more than at first appears.' Suddenly
He arose, 'It is my wish that I shall accompany
You to Bekelert, I have not been there for a long
While, 'tis time I laid to rest my sorrow, the wrong
Of years ago cannot be changed, but in such a place
One should rejoice, not avoid. With your good grace
We will go now, the hunting can await another day.'
As the two tried to hide their concern and dismay
They went out into the sunlight, where the Prince
Was issuing orders, in preparation for his absence.
'I will return tomorrow, for the journey is but short
Enjoy a day of leisure, there will be time yet for sport.'

The Reunion

The three men walked in silence alongside the Glaslyn river
Rejoicing in the solitude and peace of the hills, with heather
Clad slopes and tall trees bending down to the waters edge,
White foam broke over the grey stones, creating a ledge
For the travellers to walk along. Stopping to take a drink
The Prince spoke to Gwyhyr 'I have great cause to think
Since I met with you, your tale of olden days, of legends
From our past, carried the ring of truth, as of old friends
That you knew, yet how could that be, for many centuries
Have past since the all mighty Guorthigern and his armies
Lived in these lands. Our young knight, whose journey
Began at my command, now carries an aura of destiny,
The carefree boy has become a man in so short a time.'
'He has but one more mountain in his journey to climb,
If he succeeds where others have failed, and lays to rest
Sorely tried souls, then his quest will be most blessed,
And an inspiration to all that come after. I have belief
In his integrity, but fear that greed may make a thief
Of others.' Gwyhyr looked full hard into the eyes
Of Llewelyn, who filled with anger, began to rise
And turned towards the older man. 'Do not measure
Me against other men, whatever your fears, I assure
You nothing is great enough to tempt me to become
As a common varlet, I will not take of their own from
Any man, not even if the fabled Myrddyn's treasure
Had been found.' Suddenly he ceased, a look of pure
Delight crossed his face, 'The cave under the hillside,
Waiting for a fair-headed youth, many times I've tried
To find its hidden entrance, listened for its bell to toll
Yet never found the door. I beg you, tell me the whole
Story.' He listened intently as Rhydian related the story,

141

Telling how he found the cave where was held the gaudy
Casket and its simply wrapped contents, leaving the gold
Untouched, had taken the scabbard to Gwyhyr, who foretold
The dangers it would bring. So intent were the three
They did not hear a sharp intake of breath from the tree,
Lined banks behind them, nor see the figure of a man
Hidden in the shadows. 'And now my friends, what plan
Do you have for your precious burden? You are entrusted
With a sacred bequest, if this is known you will be hunted
To your death.' 'I put my faith in God that he will guide
Me to safety and show me the final resting place to hide
The sword and its scabbard. But enough, I see the raven
Flies overhead, 'tis time to move onwards to where Gwen
Awaits us.' Continuing down the river bank, each deep
In thought, unaware of their follower, down the steep
Path out of the ravine. Swiftly they passed through
Bekelert, reaching the Priory as the bell called the few
To prayer, their shadow drawing closer, keeping tight
To the walls. Through the gate Rhydian beheld a sight
That caused him to laugh out loud. A youth chased
Three hound pups round a destrier, belongings strewed
Around a pack pony, panniers resting under her belly
Contents fallen on the grass under the shade of a tree.
Before the wind blew them further, a young maid tried
Hastily to retrieve them whilst the playful pups carried
Them to far parts of the Abbey grounds. 'See my Lord
What manner of army this knight leads, a fabled sword
Could not have a more unlikely guard.' At the sound
Of his voice Gwen turned and ran with the hound
Cyfaill towards him. Cadair whinnied, and pulled
Young Alain over, as towards Rhydian, he too, headed,
Who was knocked to the ground by the assorted mêlée.
Llewelyn bent down to pick up a pup from the fray,
'You have the finest followers any could wish for,
I envy you them. I would that others looked to your

142

Choice of companions. The cenau are strong and bold
This one reminds me of my Gelert, whose tale I told
You before.' His hand caressed the soft head, sorrow
Bringing a tear to his eye. 'My lord, he is yours, allow
Me to present him to you, his sire is of great Phinn's
Lineage, his dam here saved my life with her brains,
So he is worthy to be a Prince's friend.' With order
Restored once more they entered the Priory cloister.

The Evening

The quiet of the hall was broken by the excited voices
Of reunited lovers, exchanging tales and gentle kisses,
With greeting old friends and making new, until finally
Ceasing, then peace descended once more to the Priory.
Rhydian watched Cadair and Bronn grazing on the banks
Of the Glaslyn, caressing Cyfaill's head as he gave thanks
For the safe arrival of his beloved friends, wondering
If he had the right to ask them to continue, for leading
Them to the journey's end would bring many dangers.
Deep in thought, he remained unaware of the stranger's
Footfall behind him, unheeding of his hound's warning.
He returned to his friends with the evening sun setting
Below the mountain, bathing the Priory in a crimson
Glow, as if the very stones were afire, a true beacon
To all who travelled the lonely roads. The low murmur
Of voices sounded in his ears, coming from the arbour
Where the scent of herbs lay gentle on the warm air.
Seating himself on the grass at Gwen's feet, his fair
Head resting on her knee, Rhydian began to talk
To his Prince, of his adventures, his flight as a hawk,
How Cyfaill and Cadair rescued him, meeting Alain
And Gwen. He told him of his joust, of the shame
When he failed in the last moment of victory, unable
To land the final blow. Of truth intermixed with fable.
As he drew to a close, his eyelids drooping in sleep,
He said to Llewelyn 'I place my trust in you, to keep
These words close, and if I fail in my final task, I plead
That you take care of my Lady.' 'There will be no need
I would not leave your side, for together we journey.
I know not where you are going, but you go with me.'
Llewelyn looked at Gwen, a smile crossing his face,
'I give my word, I am honoured that I have a place

In your story, it is a sacred charge, I will not fail you
None shall hear from me of your precious treasure,
Nor do I covet it. I have received a greater reward,
That of your friendship. But take heed, you must guard
Well the burden you carry, until the Annwen once more
Have it in their keeping.' Turning towards the door
The prince left them, his new pup held tight in his arm.
'Before we retire, one thing worries me, I hope no harm
Has come to the smallest pup, only three arrived here.'
'Do not fret, she is well, but still small. She is in the care
Of Ythel, he loves her dearly and she is safe with him.'
They all returned to their rooms not aware that a slim
Figure emerged from hiding and stood in the shadow
Staring at the windows of the Priory. 'I now will follow
Your every step until I can at last take my revenge for
Deeds of long ago. My forefather suffered and swore
One day to return to reclaim that which was rightfully
His. I will redeem that oath, so all the truth shall see!'

Onwards

Once inside the Priory, Llewelyn held fast to Rhydian,
Keeping him back, 'Take heed of this, there is a man,
His name is Sir Medraut, that travels with my company.
I care not for him, for methinks he is not trustworthy,
Although he comes from an ancient line. This morn
He asked me many questions, where you were born,
Who your father is, why you travelled as a commoner
With such strange company, I gave him no answer.
You must hide well your treasures, for I am minded
This man has some knowledge, you are forewarned.'
In the quiet of his room Rhydian took his coat, ripping
It open to remove the leather scabbard, then placing
This in Bronn's pannier curling it under a Hessian cover
Deep in the bottom, on this laid Aldan's blanket over,
To make a soft bed for the pups to lie on. He pondered
About the sword Caledfwlch, it must be concealed
But how? Taking his crwth, he bound the sword tight
Against its back, the blade lying flat along the upright
Bar, then lashed it firmly to the saddle roll that would
Lie across Bronn's broad back. Taking his own sword
He wrapped this in plain cloth, its shape telling all
What lay within. The sunlight of dawn lit up the hall
Before he finished, satisfied he laid down to sleep,
His mind filled with concern for that in his keep.
Next day they bade farewell to Prince Llewelyn,
'I would go with you, but I must return, for within
My knights are many who wish to take my place
If I am gone for long, you may see another face
Ruling my land. May God's blessings go with you.'
They watched him leave, the small body of his new
Hound tucked inside his jacket. A feeling of great
Sadness filled Rhydian, it was as if a heavy weight

Was pulling down his heart. He needed guidance
More than ever, yet he was left wanting, and once
Again he was alone, where were his mentors now?
He felt a soft hand slip into his, he laughed, for how
Could he be lonely, with Gwen and Alain by his side?
Together with his horse and hounds they would ride
Through any storm that approached, showing no fear
Or doubt and grow in love and stature without peer.

Towards The Llŷn

Rhydian scanned the blue sky hoping for sight
Of a black bird high in the sky circling right
Above them, striving to hear the harsh craa
Of its call, but in the air all was still for as far
As he could see. They followed the Glaslyn
As it flowed to the open sea close by, the Llŷn,
That narrow strip of land pointing westward
To their journey's end. The path was hard
And narrow, rocks, slippery with wet moss
Underfoot, letting only the surefooted across.
They left the riverside, climbing higher to seek
An easier way, where Cadair's great physique
And Bronn's heavy load could move with speed
In safety, they continued onward, with no need
For rest. The valley's beauty spread out before
Them, the bright, crashing water creating a roar
As it fell down waterfalls, that could be heard
From their lofty pathway. Above a lonely bird,
Like a sentinel, pointing to where the distant sea
Beckoned tempting the river onwards, to bravely
Enter the big ocean tides, never more to tumble
Over the mountains of its youth. Reaching a coastal
Track they descended to the moryd, where a bridge
Crossed onto flat, fertile land over a sandy ridge,
Where lay small boats awaiting for the next tide.
Fishermen watched the strangers as they arrived
Warily at first, then seeing no threat, in friendship.
Children laughed at the pups as they began to slip
Down Bronn's back to run free, their legs, cramped
From the long confine of the pannier collapsed,
Leaving them at the mercy of small hands eager
To catch and hold them tight. Through the laughter

Came a louder voice, asking to know from whence
The party came, and to where they travelled hence.
A tall figure walked towards them, by his bearing
A true man of the sea, his skin bronzed with living
Under the sun, eyes gazing from a weather-beaten
Face, Rhydian knew that here was a leader of men.
'We travel to the Llŷn, firstly to Borth-y-Gest where
My lady's father set sail to lands unknown, to the fair
Country that Prince Madoc found. Her brother sailed
Too and has ne'er been seen again, she has desired
To see once again the place from which they left.'
The man stared long at Rhydian, 'That is but the heft
Of the tale, I choose to ask no more, for I can judge
A man's worth, now eat with us, do not begrudge
Me the pleasure of your company, I become lonely
For new tales.' That day they were treated as royalty
A feast prepared from the sea, cooked on an open fire
Washed down by homebrewed ale, none could desire
Better company. At Gwen's behest, Rhydian began to sing
Until the night drew in and reluctantly children, hiding
From sight, were gathered up and an evening of magic
Ended. From afar a man watched, his mind becoming sick
With envy at the easy camaraderie with which Rhydian
Made friends, his heart filled with bitterness and poison
With the desire to take from him that which he valued
And held dear. He would bide his time, until unguarded,
The treasures he would take and regain his rightful place
As a Prince in the land his forefathers once ruled, erase
The wrongs of years ago. Keeping these thoughts close
He settled down to the dark sleep where shadow blows
The daylight away, and so creates frightening dreams.
The dawn broke to a grey and dismal day, no beams
Of sun broke through the mist curling in from the sea
Hiding the water's edge from view, where the boggy
Land could entrap an unwary traveller holding tight

149

Until the tide turned, and so be lost forever from sight.
'Keep close to the hillside, do not stray off the shore
And you will be safe. Follow the land, it may take more
Miles, but guideless, the treath must not be crossed.'
With this warning the fisherman bid farewell, tossed
His nets into the boat and set sail. Taking good heed
Of his words the small party left, Cyfaill took the lead
Her keen nose testing the air and her innate instinct
Choosing the right path. Following them, as if linked
By an invisible cord, came the lone knight. Running
Quickly and easily, the many years of hard training
Had given him speed and endurance, he maintained
To keep them well in sight. By noon they had reached
Pen Morfa, where they stopped to rest, yet an uneasy
Fear held Rhydian, he could not be still. 'I must see
What lies beyond, this place holds old knowledge
Crying out to be heard, with words in a language
I can feel but not understand.' He rode Cadair fast
Away, to a hilltop, where trees grew thickly, past
Green meadows, until he entered a grove of oak
With mistletoe hanging from branches like a cloak
Behind which no birds sang. Dismounting he stood
Straight, his eyes closed, and mind open. A flood
Of voices rang in his ears, chanting incantations,
Entering his senses, no longer words, but emotions,
Pure feelings, that overcame him. Suddenly all ceased.
A soft silver light took the shape of an old wizened
Man who held out his hand to Rhydian, as they touched
He felt a cold fire spread through his body, he watched
As the light curled around him, until the two were as one.
Slipping into a deep sleep the sound of song had begun
To enter his spirit, unknown words from an ancient past,
Bringing peace and tranquillity, yet full of power, a fast
Flowing stream washing over him, cleansing his mind.
While he slept time seemed halted, he saw unconfined

Across the years from beyond the grave to the distant
Future, feeling the common thread that bound all sentient
Beings. Slowly he woke, Cadair stood guard, sides heaving
With sweat, his eyes full of fear, yet no thought of leaving
His beloved master entered his being. Rhydian reached out
To touch his friend, a new understanding, no more doubt
Of his chosen course, giving him the courage to continue
Onward, to reject the temptation of great power, that few
Could resist. As he approached Pen Morfa the sun broke
Through, as if the heavens rejoiced in new found hope.

Borth-y-Gest

They soon reached Borth-y-Gest, the road was easy
And untroubled, here the small harbour was busy
With boats of all sizes, some large enough to sail
To far distant lands, whilst others were small, frail
Craft for skimming over the marshlands, their flat
Keel drawing little water, propelled by poles that
Skilfully saw them glide among the reeds, hunting
The wildfowl, laying traps for unwary game to bring
Home. Gwen looked around her, brow furrowed
As she recalled that day from her past, she had fled
From her mother's side, clasping her brother tight
Pleading with him to stay, not to leave that night.
She could feel still her father's arms, iron strength,
As he pulled her away, then carrying her the length
Of the boat, placing her harshly in Aldan's embrace.
In her despair she wept, tears running down her face
She watched her beloved Bron leave her life forever.
Now she stood in the same place, a younger brother
At her side. 'You were but a babe, I was not unkind,
I loved you full well, but I would have left all behind
To go with them. Our mother would not leave you,
Nor this land, and I was only a girl-child. I often rue
This day, but no more, for I have found a true love
In my Rhydian, and in you, Alain, I could not have
A better, truer, brother. I thank you for bringing me
Here, I have chased away the demons, they now flee
My life for ever.' Then turning away from the harbour
She sat on a low wall gazing far along the foreshore.
Rhydian knelt at her feet, 'I cannot promise that your
Life will be one of ease, of wealth I have nothing, I am poor
In all but love, but this I swear, as long as there is breath
In my body I will hold your heart in mine, until my death.'

152

Gwen gently touched his face, 'I want no earthly riches
For I have the wealth of friends, so no more speeches,
Whilst the sun is still high, we will take the road west
And move on, for we have yet to complete our quest.'

To Carn Fadryn

Leaving the harbour behind they climbed the headland
Where they could see to the distant horizon. Like a hand,
The Llŷn pointed their way, disappearing into the misty
Clouds that hung over the high hills. They saw the newly
Built walls of Llewellyn's castle perched on top of a small
Hill, almost an island, across the bay, the twin towers, tall
And strong, stood their guard. The party, keeping a goodly
Distance from the castle, followed the path of the saintly
Cadfan to the Isle of Ynis Enlli, where many had found
Solace and healing after crossing the treacherous sound
From Aberdaron. They met with other travellers along
The way, stopping at St Cawrdraf's church, here a throng
Of pedlars greeted them, selling sweetmeats and fairings.
Rhydian, aware of the dangers that such a crowd brings,
Carried on without stopping until they came to a quiet
Place by a river. In the balmy evening, the warm firelight
Casting a glow around the makeshift camp, they rested.
'I dreamt I was a hawk that flew high above this blessed
Land. Down below I saw the sea on either side of a crest
Of hills that ran down to its tip. I saw a fort, holding fast
To the stone-covered moors, I felt drawn to that place
As if someone was calling to me – now I wish to retrace
My flight and find the fort once more. We must leave
The Pilgrims Way and take the inland path, for I believe
That on that lonely hill there are answers to be found.'
As they slept on in peace, their watcher made no sound
To show his presence, biding his time till he was ready
To act. That morn they left the flat coastal plain for hilly
Moors, which offered no cover for their shadow to hide.
He was content to stay back, keep to the lower hillside
For he knew they had to descend the ridge en route
To the Island, watching, as they searched for the fort.

Carn Fadryn

The bleak moorland that covered Carn Fadryn contrasted
With the green fertile land below, from its wind blasted
Summit Rhydian saw the world beneath lie like a picture,
Splashes of green and yellow, encircled by the sea, pure
Blue flecked with white. Behind him Eryri's tall mountains
Reached to the sky. Southwards, rivers meet the ocean's
Waves as they flow into the wide bay. Beyond the distant
Horizon lies the land of the Tuatha-de-Danann, an ancient
People whose spirits live on in the otherworld. Ruined walls
Lay all around, a mighty fort had once stood here, it calls
Out to those who will listen, telling of the hopes and fears
Of times past, now and the future, memories of forebears
That lie deep within the soul. Gwen moved beside him
With the cool air causing a shiver to ripple along her slim
Body, his thoughts returned to shelter before the night
Drew in. Together they found a place, where, as the light
Began to fade they made camp, the fire created shadows,
Giving life to the stones around them. As the moon rose
A plaintive song drifted on the breeze, waking Rhydian
From fitful slumber. Following the music he saw a man
Standing on the ridge, staring out to sea, where a great
Wave thundered over an unknown land, a watery fate
Descending on Maes Gwyddno. As he watched the sea
Appeared to move with the song, when, from the briny
Foam, burst forth horses, pure white and glistening under
The moonlight, so swift they outran the sea, the thunder
Of their hooves awakening the sleeping villages, calling
Them to flight. As he listened the music was changing
Becoming fast, louder and more urgent, a cry of despair
Torn from the man's soul. As if in answer to this prayer
A black bolt descended from the sky, wings held tightly
To its side, the familiar sight of a raven dived to the sea,

Disappearing into the maelstrom. A horse, black as jet,
Galloped out of the water, eyes like the yellow sunset
Staring from his giant head. Flying fast over the ground,
He came to a lonely dyke, where the great earth mound
Bravely held back the incoming waters. Like a cauldron,
A deep well boiled and churned, there a young maiden
Stood by the wall, tears of shame flowing down her face
As she tried to mend the breaking bank. From this place
The horse took her, running to the far distant high land
There, exhausted, he sank to the earth. From the upland
She looked on in sorrow, as all but a few were drowned,
Overcome by the crashing sea. From his hill a spellbound
Singer cried bitter-sweet tears, his song now a low lament
For the lost. The dawn slowly broke, returning the present
To the hilltop where Rhydian stood. At this time the
   Annwn
Is close to those who open their eyes and hearts, too soon
The portal closes, but for a moment, standing in a gateway,
Two figures looked across time, their love speeding its way,
Enfolding him in peace. As the vision faded he wondered
At its meaning, of questions that needed to be answered.

The Attack

As the morning sun rose over the windblown hilltop
Rhydian wandered slowly among the rocky outcrop,
His thoughts still with the visions of the night before.
In the distance, where the land ran into the sea, he saw
A green island that beckoned him, surrounded by white
Flecked waves dancing over the water. A shaft of light
Lay across the flat fields below, as if pointing the way,
A sign, or mayhap a portent from a watching Faye.
Turning to go, his foot caught a fallen stone bringing
Him to his knees. He brushed the dust away revealing
Ancient carvings, half-broken fragments of forgotten
Words. *Hic jacet*, here lies, *pace*, peace, as he read on
Understanding came to him, *Matercula*, little mother,
The names *Sevira* and *Modrom*, he could see another
Word, still clear – *liberta*. A caressing warmth spread
Up his arm, entwining itself in his heart, a pure thread
Of love reaching across the years. 'Be easy my Roman
Soldier, the Lady Elen took care of your child, you can
Rest in peace now.' Then with a light spirit he returned
To his lady, ready for the next part of the quest, renewed
In vigour and purpose, eager to continue on the journey.
As they descended the steep hillside, waiting patiently,
Their lone watcher was biding his time, ready to strike.
Once on level ground, Rhydian charged Alain to make
Camp in the lush meadows yonder, where the grazing
And water was plentiful, then he took Cyfaill hunting.
They set a quick pace until they were soon out of sight.
After an hour of good hunting they rested, the sunlight
Warming them they began to doze, suddenly the hound
Gave tongue, waking Rhydian, with one great bound
She was flying back to camp, all other thought chased
Out of her mind. As he followed he heard the raised,

157

Fearful call of Cyfaill, urging him forward. As he neared
The place of their parting he saw Alain, so still he feared
For his life, Bronn stood guard, then a pup began to whine.
Rhydian searched, but of Cadair and Gwen there was no sign

The Melée

Rhydian tended to Alain, washing the blood from his face
Desperate to know what had happened at this place,
Praying for life to return to the motionless body. Slowly
Alain began to move, his unfocused gaze staring blindly
Upwards. The fog began to lift from his mind and words
Tumbled out 'He has Gwen and Bronn is hurt, the sword's
Thrust slashed her deeply. I tried, but he was too strong
I failed you.' Tears welling unchecked, he took a long
Sobbing breath. Looking at Bronn, there was no sign
Of a wound, just the faintest of marks, a pale white line
Across her chest. 'She still wears her panniers, fear not
The scabbard protects all living creatures, now tell what
Has befallen Gwen.' 'You had no sooner gone from sight
Than a man appeared, so silent and swift, I did not fight,
There was no time before he held Gwen, I was afeared
He would harm her. The pup bit him, then Cadair reared
And in the melee Gwen broke free, falling to the ground
She hit her head and lay still, I tried to move, but found
I could not, it was as if my legs were held tight, bound
Together by fear. By the time my courage had returned
It was too late, he stood over her, his sword unsheathed.
Then without thought I ran at him, but he only laughed
At me and thrust me away, then he slashed Bronn, I saw
Blood flowing and flew at him, I remember no more.'
Rhydian looked at Alain, laid his hand on his shoulder
'Be not ashamed for many men, well trained and older
Know what it is to be powerless to move when the heat
Of battle descends.' Standing deep in thought, the beat
Of his heart pounding hard in his body, he pondered
His next move. 'We must follow them, the tracks lead
Towards the sea, but I do not understand, I am the only
One who Cadair will obey, then why has this man freely

Taken him?' Alain saw the look of pain, of betrayal
On Rhydian's face. 'He has gone with Gwen, a loyal
Guard to protect her, see also, a small dog's paw prints
Following them, Cyfaill's son is a true warrior methinks.
She'll have no trouble tracking them, we can travel fast.'
Rhydian began to smile, with his spirits lifting at last.

The Rescue Begins

Rhydian removed Aldan's blanket from Bronn's pack,
Placing it around the shivering Alain's slender back.
'Your mother's love will give protection, her courage
Will sustain you in whatever lies ahead, her knowledge
Of healing is an ancient craft from an ancient people.'
From its hiding place he took Caledfwlch, 'The fable
Of this sword grew in my mind throughout childhood
I dreamt of wearing it into battle, now when I should,
I feel a strange reluctance, for it has a malignant power
That I fear may overcome me. But I must not cower
Behind my fancies.' With sword and scabbard united
Once more, they followed Cyfaill as she eagerly sped
After the trail, heading west towards the setting sun,
Bronn carrying her burden steadily towards the barren
Slopes of Mynydd Rhiw. The sky burned like a fiery
Furnace, a crimson land surrounded by a golden sea
Out of which rose a dark brooding hill. Rhydian halted
Bronn, and softly called Cyfaill to his side, he pointed
To where figures could be seen, sheltering in the lee
Of the hill 'You must bide here, I will travel quietly
Alone.' Alain began to protest 'I wish to go alongside
You, she is my sister.' Understanding, Rhydian smiled
'I may not succeed in the task, you must keep a vigil
If I fail, take up the challenge. Who knows what peril
Lies in store. Cyfaill will stay here also, her keen senses
Will tell you if help is needed, for I make no pretences
To fighting skills, I may yet call you to my assistance.'
Alain watched as they vanished into the distance
Sadly he settled down to wait, unsure of his desires,
Should Rhydian succeed alone? Or should his squire's
Help be asked for? Stroking the soft coat of his puppy

As she slept beside him he began his long vigil, barely
Breathing, making no noise, listening for the call to glory
That would give him a high place in a true knight's story.

The Rescue

The evening sky glowed as if Beltane's fire lingered
As the last rays of the setting sun threw bright red
Layers over the menacing hills, slowly fading into
Half-light, till the cool silver moon washed it anew.
Into this shadow land Rhydian slipped, his mind
Taking control, stilling the beating heart, to find
A route to take, unseen, towards the menacing
Slopes of Mynydd Rhiw. There in the lingering
Light he saw Gwen, she sat so still and quiet
That he feared for her safety, he was beset
With self doubt, was he truly a brave knight
Fit to rescue his lady? Did he have the right
To wear the sword of destiny? He watched
As across the scene a tall dark figure moved,
In his hand was Rhydian's own sword, now loose
Of its cover. In great anger he raised his voice
And approached Gwen. At this Rhydian, all caution
Forgotten, started forward he began to quicken
His pace, calling her name, sending a warning
To her captor. The man turned round, facing
The oncoming youth with a smile of anticipation
On his lean face. He spoke softly, 'I was certain
You would follow, I will take that which is rightly
Mine, you fooled me once, but not again, I see
Caledfwlch by your side, no doubt that shabby
Scabbard is what I seek also. Come here my pretty
Boy and I will show you how a real man can fight.'
Rhydian stood very still, keeping Gwen in his sight,
Answering softly 'You are not the first to call me boy
Come closer and find the truth, for it will give me joy
To prove you wrong, you have done harm to those
I hold dear, for this you must pay.' They drew close,

163

Each wary to strike first, Medraut's sword flickered
Like a silver tongue, as his practiced eye measured
The distance between them, his lithe body swaying
As he circled around the younger knight, standing
So still, biding his time, content to wait, the great
Caledfwlch, heavy in his hand, seemed to pulsate
With power, urging him to fight. Then, with a sudden
Move he lunged forward, fighting as if a demon
Lived inside his body, until time itself stood still.
He forgot where he was or who he was, until,
His enemy lying helpless at his feet, he raised
His arms above his head. As a red mist glazed
His eyes, he stood poised for the final thrust.
As the arm descended, Medraut felt the last
Of life slipping away, eyes closed he waited.
He did not see the gentle hand that stayed
The blow, nor hear the soft voice of calm
Cooling the battle fired mind with its balm.
Slowly feeling the madness of rage depart,
Rhydian saw her sweet face clearly, his heart
Filled with love, he bent down to his defeated
Foe and spoke softly 'My fair lady has pleaded
For your life and so you live, now go in peace.'
Medraut arose, not understanding his release,
Unable to speak, he stood looking at Rhydian
Seeking an answer, but for him there was none.

Gwen's Reason

Holding his lady close Rhydian sought comfort
From her presence, bringing peace to his fraught
Thoughts, her love calming his disordered mind
Until all anger left him, yet still he could not find
In his heart forgiveness. 'You stayed my hand,
I would know the reason why,' he was unmanned
And at my mercy.' For a while Gwen gave no
Answer, slowly she spoke, 'It seemed as though
You were no longer the man I loved, a different
Person lived inside your body, for one moment
I had lost you, if you killed that defeated knight
You would become as they were, using might
To conquer. I wanted my perfect, gentle, lover
To return to me.' 'Your wisdom is from another
Time. I felt all-powerful, as if no one could harm
Me, the world was mine to command. My arm
Wielded a great weapon, its life force beyond
My control, until it is part of me, and I respond.
It is an evil thing, the scabbard too, for no man
Can resist them, they must be taken to a haven
Where they will be hidden for ever from sight.'
Then he wrapped the scabbard and sword tight
In its plain cloth, seeming no more than an old
Saddle roll. 'I must know, for you have not told
Me, did Medraut touch you?' He could not look
Gwen in the eyes, his colour mounted, he took
A deep breath, waiting for her reply. Laughingly
She answered, 'Cadair would not let him near me
And my little warrior pup bit him, he regretted
Taking me and Cadair long before you arrived.
Come let us return to my brother, for his vigil
Will seem long alone, then at dawn we travel.'

165

Part Six
Journey's End

To Ynys Enlli

The morning dawned to a grey and dismal sky
A fine misty veil of rain hung over the nearby
Trees. In the distance the grey sky merged into
The angry sea where white tipped waves threw
Their cold water onto the shore, creating vast
Lakes where grassland lay, echoes from the past
Rang in Rhydian's ears, fearfully he scanned
The horizon. 'We must keep to the higher land
The sea is restless, Annwn's gates may yet open.'
The wind grew stronger as they took uncertain
Steps through unknown pathways to Ynys Enlli.
Rain began to fall in heavy bursts, unable to see
They followed the path westward to Aberdaron,
To the pilgrims church of St Hywyn, a beacon
On the sands for those who made the crossing
Over the sound. But today there was no sailing
To the island of saints, the boats were beached
On the deserted shore, as great waves reached
The stone walls of the church, its foundations
Buried deep under the sand, defying the actions
Of the sea. To the wet and weary travellers
It was a welcome sight. 'I regret that my purse
Is light, I will seek the Abbot, I have the letter
From Llewelyn, his hand may stretch this far.'
Leaving his friends he entered the small church.
Sat on a stone chair, like an old bird on its perch,
Was a small figure, white hair forming a halo
Round his head. 'Enter Sir Rhydian, I know
Who you are and why you are come, my friend
Here has told me of your travels he will attend
To your companions.' He beckoned to a dimly

Lit corner, where two bright eyes knowingly
Stared out, swiftly followed by the black sleek
Shape of Menw. With joy Rhydian began to speak
'I have missed you, and began to wonder if old
Friends had deserted me. Yet I have been told
That I need not worry, help will be there when
I need it most. I crave your assistance for Gwen,
She has need of food and shelter, the others too.'
'You are honoured young man, for only a few
Men gain the trust of an Eiddlig Gor. Come sit
Here on the chair of peace, an honour you are fit
To take. I have a message to pass, now heed me
Carefully.' They sat in silence as the old seer
Gathered his thoughts. 'This storm will last
For days, and then the seas will run too fast
For fishermen to risk the sound. Now is the time
For you to go, tomorrow morning before Prime
You can be on a boat sailing across that sea
Where others will be waiting on Ynys Enlli.
You must go alone, this journey is your destiny
To decide without aid or hinder. You are free
To turn back now, for none will stop you, take
Your Lady home, take your rewards and make
Her content. Or take the last step of your quest,
Its ending in your hands though it may yet be wrest
From you.' With his head high and eyes steady
Rhydian replied 'Show me the boat for I am ready.'

The Crossing

The sky was dark and grey, letting no sunlight through,
The wind blew hard throwing the sea around, as though
A mighty battle was taking place far beneath the waves
That crashed over the rocky coast, forming those caves
Where sea monsters lie hidden, guarding the gateways
To the otherworld. 'Gwen, you must leave ere the day's
Course is run, there is a goodwife nearby who will give
You and Alain shelter until my return, for tonight I live
As a knight at vigil and prepare for whatever the morn
Shall bring me. I am to make myself ready before dawn
So now we must say farewell. I have a gift, to bestow
Made with rare skill and I believe, love, from long ago.'
He placed among her long dark hair the circlet of gold,
So long forgotten in its secret place, hidden in the cold
Mine shaft. Gwen untied a leather thong that lay around
Her neck taking from it the ring of Emrys. 'I have found
It has warmth, unlike normal stone, bringing me comfort.
I give it back to you, my talisman in battles to be fought.'
Later he was woken from fitful slumber and collecting
His crwth and pack he quietly left the church, following
Menw's flight, down a steep, narrow path to an inlet.
Rhydian saw a man, face half covered by a cowl, yet
Strangely familiar. He spoke 'Come aboard my young
Friend, you will be safe with me this time.' He flung
Back his hood, to show Gwyhyr's keen, far-seeing eyes.
'I do not sail this craft, Barrinthus, the ferryman, is wise
In the currents around the Island of Saints, he can ride
The waters as no other. On dry land I will be your guide.'
Barrinthus, holding the tiller in one hand, the sail stay
In the other, signed to Gwyhyr, pushing them away
From the shore and straightway into the seething sea.

171

Finding a path under the waves where none should be
The ferryman sailed the boat safely across the sound
Speaking not a word. Approaching the isle he found
A sheltered place to land, then his passengers ashore
He turned back. Words that it seemed the wind bore,
Drifted past Rhydian, 'God speed, God bless' so quiet
He hardly heard them, so deep he would not forget.

On Ynys Ennli

In silent companionship the two friends
Walked towards the Isle's higher lands
Through the orchards where the Abbey's
Sheep grazed amongst the apple trees,
They followed the path that encircled
The hill. The sun's light slowly touched
Grey clouds, dark and threatening above
A brooding sea, lightening a rocky cove.
On this weed-covered shore they rested
Beside a stream, the clear fresh water fed
A shallow hollow in the stone. Kneeling
Down to take a drink from the refreshing
Pool, Rhydian saw the surface move, as if
A tiny storm blew, a picture grew, a cliff
Rising from the sea, where ancient stone
Steps led to a well. Here sitting all alone,
Was a young maid watching as the ebbing
Tide revealed Ffynnon Fair, whose cleansing
Powers had sustained many a pilgrimage
To Ynys Enlli. He drank deeply, her image
Etched on his mind, a talisman to protect
And guide him as he faced the final aspect
Of his journey. 'I must leave you to return
Before Prime, the Augustinians are stern
In their ways, I am their guest and so abide
By their rules.' His face filling with pride,
Gwyhyr laid his hand upon the young man's
Shoulder. 'You have a wisdom that spans
Across the ages, I trust you to take the right
Course, may God be with you, carry his light
High and you will find a safe route to follow,
As the ebbing tide recedes a bridge will show

Lying just beneath the waves. You must cross
In haste, for a short time there is an egress
In the rock, a portal to where, I do not know.
Here you must enter, whilst the water is low,
Before the tide turns and the rising sea covers
The entrance once more. The Abbey Brothers
Await me, I will keep watch and pray for you.'
Sitting on the rocks, waiting as the dawn drew
Nigh, Rhydian travelled back to those carefree
Days at home, when adventure was but a story
To dream about, battles were as yet unfought
And love lay waiting to be found. He thought
Of the sword that lay in his grasp, of the power
That it could bring, of the glory that its wearer
Could find. He felt once more that heady moment
When the victory was his, when life or death meant
Which way his blade had fallen. Holding the sword
As it lay by his side, he arose and walked toward
The sea, where through the grey light of daybreak
He saw a figure, still and quiet, watching him make
His way to the shore. With long black hair flowing
Down to a slender waist, framing a face of glowing
Beauty, from which two dark blue eyes smouldered
With desire. She raised her arms high and revealed
A body, lithe and sinuous swaying to unheard music,
He was drawn unresisting to her, letting the rhythmic
Dance drown him in sensuous pleasure. She laughed
Softly, entwining him in her embrace, her witchcraft
Holding him in thraldom, she laid claim to his soul,
His mind, and for her use alone, his heart she stole.

The Immortal Choice

As the waves crashed onto the shore, the wind howled
Unheard, around their heads then time itself was stilled.
She laughed, soft, yet triumphant, laden with promises
Of pleasure to come, of unknown delights and wishes
To be fulfilled, she raised her arms, and at her command
The storm abated and an unearthly quiet covered the land.
Into this dreamlike world Rhydian followed, all resistance
Gone, moving further into her embrace, held in a trance
From which he had neither the power, nor desire to break
Free, his blood ran hot with a lust that naught could slake.
Her face held between his hands he gazed, wonderingly,
Into her eyes 'By what name are you known? Your beauty
Is not of mortals, yet I hold and touch you, your caresses
Stir my innermost being, leaving me bereft of all senses.'
'Do you not know of me? Look deep inside your heart,
Have you not dreamed of me since childhood? My art
Has grown over the eons, my favours bestowed on few
Men, for only the bravest can match me. I am Nimue,
I am Viviane, I am Modron, I am Ninniane, I am Le Faye.'
The rising sun caught her with the golden beams of day
Bathing her in light until she became as one with the sky.
Standing in her reflected glory his dreams began to fly
Into the realms of history, to where the knights of old
Rode out to fight demons from the dark side of the world.
The being beside him began to move, away from the sea,
Away from the pathway under the waves, away from the
Journey's end. Rhydian followed, held by invisible cords
That bound him as surely as a silken rope, going onwards
To a new life that promised him power and immortality.
With each slow step he took he felt the blood run coldly
In his veins, all warmth was draining from him, leaving
Nothing but coldness in its place. He tried to halt, fearing

To go on but she was so strong, her hand seemed melded
To his, as if she was becoming him, he felt a great dread
And prayed for help, seeking from his heart its innermost
Treasures to sustain him. Far away he heard singing, lost
In the air, seeking a way to reach him, his soul called back.
He chose the certainty of pure love, and rejected the black
Future of power, he chose the path of humanity, spurning
For ever the promise of glory, of immortality, so breaking
Her icy hold and setting him free to pursue his chosen way.
Once more he was alone, with nothing remaining of the faye.
The storm returned, the wind rising and the clouds shutting
Out the sun, the tide was flowing, the rising water covering
The bridgeway. Rhydian ran across, just reaching the portal
Before it was hidden from site, entering a narrow tunnel
That led into a wide, lofty cavern. He sank to the ground
And wept like a child, until, exhausted, fell into a sound
Healing sleep. The storm calmed down, bringing surcease
To the island and into Rhydian's sore heart came peace.

The Final Temptation

As Rhydian slept the sun travelled the sky until it rested high
Above the cave far below, seeking a way through, to defy
The dark, and bring warmth into its cold world. Rays of light
Spilled down from the roof, through ferns that clung tight
To the crevasses, turning the subterranean world green,
Rocks glistened with a myriad of stars, a beauty unseen
By mortal eyes for many long years. Music was created
As the rhythmic swell of the ocean's waves pounded
Along the shore, rousing Rhydian from his deep sleep.
He gazed in awe at the crystal cave around him, steep
Walls rose to the high vaulted ceiling, smooth as glass
They offered no footholds to climb, no escape, no pass
To travel through, the way back had closed, yet he felt
No fear, peace filled his mind, here no demons dwelt.
The rock face shimmered and as he watched became
Transparent, revealing another cavern, lit by a flame
Dancing over a cauldron of liquid, giving an ethereal
Glow, throwing into relief a raised altar. An imperial
Figure lay on this dais, golden crown around his head,
A shield across his breast. Rhydian gazed on the dead
King of legend, yet the blush of life remained bright
On his face, as if sleeping through a long, long, night.
Seated at his feet were two knights, leaning on their
Swords, they too were sleeping, at his head two fair
Maidens slept, their long hair like cloaks that covered
Slim bodies, spread out beside them. Rhydian dared
Not move, afraid one sound, one movement would
Break the charm. He recalled tales from his childhood,
The Isle of Avalon, the enchanted cave, the sleeping
Knights awaiting the recall to arms, to raise the King,
To bring Camelot once more to life. He realised at last
Why he was here, for now he could recreate the past,

177

Place the sword in his hand, then give him the water
Of life from the holy grail, and so bring King Arthur
To walk again amongst men. He could be a great
Man in this new order, a powerful knight, a fate
That he had long desired, for he would be creating
Legends that would echo down the ages, fighting
For truth and right against the evils that beset man,
All the lands would know the name of Sir Rhydian.

The Cavern

Heart beating fast with anticipation, Rhydian entered
The cavern, passing through the archway he faltered,
His mind uncertain, as he questioned his own desires.
He looked at the face of the sleeping King, the fires
Of ambition still burning bright within him, he stood
Beside the greatest warrior of all time. His childhood
Had filled with tales of knights and maidens, dragons
And magic, in his dreams he was one of the guardians
Of chivalry, riding out from Camelot's hall to defend
The weak and fight for right. Now, childhood behind
Him, he felt within him a new understanding grow,
Of another way, where no sword dealt the fatal blow.
Taking Caledfwlch, he looked upon on its hard, cold
Beauty, he remembered once more the powerful hold
It took of his senses, a hold that was broken by a hand
So gentle and a soft voice, by a love that could stand
Alone and defeat the evil of hate. Sheathing the sword
In its scabbard he placed it on the still chest of his Lord,
With hands clasped together in prayer. Taking the Grail
He filled it with clear spring water, now he must not fail
To complete his task. Holding the ancient stone cup fast
It begin to glow with a blue, flickering flame that cast
An icy light over Rhydian, a cleansing, healing, fire,
Like a mountain stream that washed away the mire.
Bathing his king's forehead with water, he prayed
For peace to reign, for the weapons of war to be laid
Down unused and the hand of friendship to be taken
In its place. A gust of wind blew through the cavern
Dimming all the lights, throwing him to the ground,
As he lay there, a veil of darkness fell over his mind.
He slept a dreamless, timeless sleep, no fears to wake
Him, no sounds came to disturb him, until daybreak.

Questions Answered

Rhydian awoke in the cavern, empty now save for
His own possessions. The king slept there no more,
Nothing remained except for memories, or mayhap
They were but dreams, woven by the Faye to entrap
Him in her power, or was she an illusion, dreaming?
In the dim light he saw a figure, an old man, watching
Him as he struggled to regain his senses, to gather
His disordered thoughts. Filling the chalice with water
Emrys offered the cup to Rhydian 'Refresh your spirit
And sit with me, you have many questions that it is fit
To ask of me now.' Rhydian stayed silent for moment
Holding the chalice, caressing it gently, 'This ancient
Vessel, I need to know the truth, is it the Holy Grail?
Do I hold in my hand that which men seek, yet fail
To find?' 'The cup was given to me long ago, to keep
In trust, to pass on the care to one who did not seek
Its power for their own glory, who would use it well
With loving intent. For once it held the blood that fell
From a man on a cross, whose life-force is eternal,
Taking men along the journey in answer to his call.
But – is it the Holy Grail that mankind strives to find?
No, for that all people have within, yet are too blind
To see it.' With Emrys' words, Rhydian understood
'It must be given to all people, somewhere good
Can reach out and touch them, I will leave it here
On this Isle, a place of pilgrimage where the fear
That lives inside our hearts can be washed away.'
Then he went to the spring and placed the grey
Stone chalice on a rocky ledge where the water
Flowed into it until it spilled out, running over
Stones before sinking deep into the sand below.
He looked to where a king had laid, the great hero

From legend, had he been created by the desired
Wish to become the perfect knight who had inspired
His childhood? He searched for signs, the cauldron
Of fire, the knights and maidens, there were none
To be found. 'I had in my grasp the means to restore
To life a myth. Before I began this journey I was sure
Of right and wrong, that the sword, justly used, could
Cleanse the world of evil. Yet I have been enthralled
By the power of revenge, I have felt the desire to kill
Take away all feelings of mercy and justice. To fulfil
My quest I must unite Caledfwlch with its scabbard
Then return them to their rightful place, this I vowed.
Last night I broke my oath, for his hand I left empty,
Sword forever out of reach, a choice, taken freely,
Closing for all eternity the hopes of a reborn king
Regaining his rightful place.' He ceased speaking
Waiting for Emrys to reply. The older man's answer
Was swift, 'The long rule of magic has passed over.
I have wandered for many years unable to leave
My mortal life, your wisdom sets me free. I believe
There are troubled times ahead, it will be a long
Hard road for man to travel, where the strong
Must lead until they find a way to live in peace.'
They sat together in silence, until feeling release
Within their heart. 'I beg you, before you depart,
To guide me for a short while longer, I must start
My return journey unsure of my welcome back
Home, for I have achieved nothing, I even lack
A place with the Prince Llewelyn, having upset
His son I am not welcome at the court. I regret
Nothing, but do not wish to re-enter my father's
House empty handed.' Emrys smiled, 'Treasures
Come in different ways, look to the knowledge
Gained, consider friendships made, the pledge
Exchanged by you and your lady, be not feared,
Your speedy return, I know, is much anticipated.'

Goodbye

Rhydian began to stir, a restlessness was upon him
A desire to move on, to leave this place whose dim
Light began to fade even more. 'I need the sunlight
Again, to feel its warmth, here it is perpetual night,
A place of peace and sanctuary, but not yet for me.'
Emrys held out his hand 'We will return to the sea
Cave, and wait until the tide shows the bridge again.
I crave your help, my powers, although they remain
With me still, are failing fast, your strength will take
Me to my friends. But before we leave I must make
This cavern and its precious content safe from harm.'
Together they left the inner cave, with his last charm
Myrddyn sealed its entrance. 'You see now a very old
Man who cannot continue without your arm to hold.'
So youth led age to the sea, as the bridge appeared
Once more. Rhydian carried Emrys until they neared
The abbey, here he paused, watching as two men
Came in greeting, with them was another, so wizen
In shape and small, like a child, yet the black eyes
Keen and knowing, told a different tale, of one wise
Of a time long ago, whose race was no more, living
Only in the stories told to while away a long evening.
Emrys embraced his boyhood friend 'Menw, the end
Is nigh, our time draws to a close. Bedwyn, you defend
The sword no more, for it now rests at peace, its power
Over men for ever gone and Gwyhyr, you are no longer
The seeker of our heir, he is here as you knew full well
When first you met. Our time is over, and we but tell
The story, at last we can now take our rest and leave
This world. A new day is dawning, we can but bequeath
Our past, our hopes and dreams to ease the hard road
Ahead.' With his heart filling with sadness, tears flowed

182

Unashamed down Rhydian's face as he listened to these
Words, 'You will live for ever, through songs and stories
Your time will be as a beacon to generations yet to come.
The trust you place in me, I have given you my solemn
Oath that I will endeavour to fulfil it, but I do not know
What it is you want from me, for I cannot land the blow
To set people free, you know that I am not a great warrior,
Who can lead men to victory. There is none with a truer
Heart than mine, I will give my own life for what is right,
And those I love, but that is not enough to take the fight
Across the land.' The four old men smiled at the golden
Youth before them. Then Menw replied 'I have spoken
With Gods and demons, my people lived at the dawning
Of men's time, have seen the strong reign, the bad bring
Fear to their realm. Through the years men and women
Who by their words and deeds have shown true vision,
Have spoken to you through dreams, for in your body
Runs their blood. Your lineage, and that of your lady,
Is rich and blessed, the hope and future lies with your
Children's children, teach them well, keep them pure
In spirit and heart, for they will travel to all climes.
When the oppressed need men of courage, in times
Of peril or paucity of spirit, your children will answer
The call, bringing wisdom and peace, to be a leader."
As Menw finished speaking, a boat came into sight,
Barrinthus once more at the helm. 'We leave tonight
Before the tide runs high, first I return across the strait
To reunite this knight with his lady, who has kept late
Hours at vigil by Ffynnon Fair and now eagerly awaits
His return.' The friends bade farewell with heavy hearts
Yet for Rhydian, with a renewed feeling of excitement
As he looked to a future filled with such good portent.

Part Seven

The
Return

Farewell

Watching from the bow of the boat Rhydian saw his friends
Fade into the distance, becoming lost in the mist that descends
Over the sea in the warmth of the rising sun. 'Farewell my true
Guides and companions, you showed me a fire's light which few
Have seen, that of the inner spirit alive in all men, I will kindle
It well in your honour and from every spark, however fragile,
Will build a mighty flame to cleanse the world in which we live.'
Barrinthus smiled at the ardent youth, 'You must first forgive
Those who do not have your strength, be their prop in times
Of doubt. The bright, fearless Llacheu lived in these climes
Many eons ago, Menw wept at his graveside and shed tears
Of blood, he too had the gift of song, passed down the years
To bring heartsease to others, use it well, it will calm anger
In any mans soul. See, – land ahead, I must return for a longer,
Final, voyage, for now five old men can rest in peace, the last
To know of the portals to Annwn. You will not be downcast,
Your lady and a long life await you.' Rhydian stepping ashore,
Turned to bid farewell to an empty sea, the boat was no more.
Gulls flew overhead, their loud cries echoing across the bay
Carrying one last thought on the wind, canu'n iach, goodbye.

Re-united

Rhydian stood in thoughtful silence, as memories swirled
  around
His mind, feelings of great sadness overwhelmed him, a
  profound
Grief for lost friendship and guidance. As he looked yearningly
Towards Ynys Enlli he heard a voice, full of love, drifting
  lightly
On the warm air, encircling him with promises yet to be
  fulfilled,
Bringing to him his future. Through eyes, wet with tears
  unshed
He saw his Gwen running with all the joyous abandon of
  youth.
As he stood laughing, she flew into his arms. 'Rhydian,
  forsooth
I do love you so, but never will I let you go away from me
  again
No matter where you go, I will go, for I am not content to
  remain
Behind, alone. Each day I sat by the holy well until the tide
  ebbed
Away, then, in the fresh spring water, I could see you. It
  seemed
You were leaving me for a far stronger passion, a powerful
  force
Had you in their thrall. I called to you, prayed that your
  choice
Would bring you once more into my keeping, I could not bear
The pain of losing you.' Gently Rhydian wiped away a tear
From her face. 'I heard you call, your love carried me through
A moment of great danger, my very soul was in peril. I renew
The vows I made, I stand before you with nothing, I spurned

188

Riches, power, and glory for an unknown future and returned
Without worldly treasures to lay before my lady, I am indeed
A failed adventurer.' Gwen smiled with pride 'Have good heed
Of me, you bring me treasure beyond price, I know of no
    man
Who could offer me that which you do, nor any other woman
On whom fortune has smiled so well.' Then, into the stillness
Came other sounds, a boy's call, pounding hooves, boisterous
Yelping of young pups, the full baying of a hound, heralding
The arrival of Alain. 'I see our private army approaching,
We must wait a short while longer for precious time alone.
In the morn we journey home, I ache to make you mine
    own.'

The Pilgrim's Road from The Llŷn

In the morn Rhydian sought the old Abbot to bid farewell,
Entering the church he saw a group in silent prayer, a bell
Tolled, its single note echoed around the nave, a dim light
Showed a figure lying before the altar, clothed in white,
Hands crossed on his chest, his beads entwined through
Fingers bent with age. Rhydian turned away for he knew
He would not receive his blessing that day, he whispered
'Godspeed, and greet my friends with love, take my word
That I will remember, for they dwell in my heart evermore.'
He left the church behind him, looking east to the shore
Where his party awaited, his stride began to lengthen.
They rode towards the rising sun, like careless children
Set free from their chores, talking, laughing they wended
Their way towards the distant mountains. They followed
The road trodden by many pilgrims, with other travellers
Going their way, telling stories, singing like troubadours
In villages as they passed by. They crossed the headlands,
They played in the sea, they rode along the golden sands
Sleeping under the stars, making friends along the way
Who gave them shelter from the rain, a dry place to stay
They worked and sang for their rewards, through the town
Of Criccieth, where the foundations of a castle were drawn
On a grassy hillock, there to take command of its estuary
As the Glaslyn swept into the sea. They rode in company,
They rode alone, following the pathways first trodden
By St Cadfan, watching the sun rise and set on the Llŷn
As each day took them further away from Ennys Enlli.
They spurned the high path from Nant-y-mor, the sea
Enticing them, behind the walls of Bryn ap Llyr's castle
Till the broad Mawddach barred their way. The gentle
Sands left behind, they turned toward Dolgellau, where
Ythel awaited them within the cloistered walls of Cymer.

Cymer Abbey Revisited

With great skill and cunning Alain and Rhydian
Hunted for game, a gift to supplement the plain
Fare of the Abbey brothers, an offering in return
For the refuge they sought. Fish wrapped in fern
Leaves, moistened with seawater thus keeping
Them fresh and sweet on the journey, a suckling
Porchell lay in Bronn's pannier, its squeals caused
Cadair to prance and snort. This much amused
Rhydian, laughing at his proud, brave destrier,
So afeared of such a tiny foe. 'It would appear
That even the strongest may have their weaker
Side, the full grown twrch is a fearsome fighter,
Many a horse will not pass by a mochen easily.
Look, the Abbey lies ahead, our friends will be
Preparing for prayers, I trust Ythel is still there
And not yet returned to Ystrad Fflur, I do desire
To talk with Brother Thomas, for I have a boon
To ask of him, we will bide here until past noon
Before we enter and make known our presence.'
They dozed in the sun of early autumn, a sense
Of well being made them content to sit at ease
Watching the river as it flowed down to the seas.
A sudden noise startled them from their slumber
A man's shadow loomed over them, 'My prayer
Has been answered, I have kept watch every day
For your return. Teg here ran fast, leading the way
To you.' Smiling he signed to a young, brindle hound
'My good friend has a keen nose, though she has found
Many a trail in the hills, she still has much to learn.'
He suddenly stopped talking, a look of great concern
Flashed across his face, he stretched his hand down
To the pup close by him, lovingly he caressed a brown

Head, wordlessly he asked a question, almost unable
To hear the answer. 'Your cenau is fair, like the fable
You have called her after, but you put me to shame
Here I have two pups, well grown but with no name
As yet!' Ythel smiled through unshed tears, all fears
Gone. 'I thought you might take Teg back, for years
I was alone, now I have friends, a home, a purpose
In my life, my soul is given to the lord, for his service,
My heart to a constant companion who gives me love
And asks nothing in return, truly I am blessed above
Other men.' With great telling of tales they entered
The abbey, where a much respected brother waited.

Old Friend

Ythel led the way through to the Abbey gardens
To a tall silent figure, who, looking in Rhydian's
Eyes gestured the seat beside him. 'Sit a while
With me, we have much to talk about.' A smile
Lit the young mans face, 'First I must ask a boon,
Of you. It is my greatest wish that you will soon
Travel to my father's house. I crave your blessing
On my wedding day, your wisdom is sustaining
Me still, during times of danger it gave me great
Strength.' 'I will be honoured, marriage is a state
Of sacred union, not to be taken lightly, your lady
Is most fortunate, or methinks tis others will envy
You such a wife. Now we will talk, time is short
I am needed yet at the infirmary, Ythel will escort
Your party to the lodging house.' Thomas listened
As the tale was told, he heard as the voice changed
In the telling, to where inner battles were fought,
And won, until he reached the answers he sought.
The young boy he first met, troubled and unsure
Had grown into a man, courageous in mind, pure
In spirit. Thomas thought about the young woman
Who had shared his journey, of the bond that ran
Between them, older than time itself, forbidden
To himself, and a fleeting regret came unbidden,
The wish to have known such love, to have sired
A son to be proud of. At this thought he chided
Himself, he had given his life into God's service
And the care of the poor. 'Ythel waits, I promise
You will be well fed tonight, although I doubt
The mochen bach is on the spit, verily his snout
Will be in the trough, the abbey farm has need
Of a new boar.' They parted, Thomas to plead

193

Forgiveness for his tardiness in visiting the sick,
Rhydian to rejoin his friends, to eat, make music
And regale all with stories of the Prince's court.
They left late the next day, giving much thought
To the meeting lying ahead, in the town of Brefi,
Did Aldan know of their journey, could she see?

Brefi

Alain seemed troubled as they rode from the Abbey
'You are strangely silent, my squire, what ails thee?'
The boy looked at Rhydian and his sister, so intent
On each other as they rode along, seeming content
With their own company. 'We have shared a fine
Adventure together, but what role will you assign
To me in your future? Will there be a place for me?'
Reaching across Bronn's broad back Rhydian gently
Rested his hand on Alain's shoulder 'I cannot tell
You how much your company means to me, I well
Recall the many times your quick wit and courage
Has saved me, can you doubt that my marriage
Will make you less to me? You will be my brother
Now, and I trust my friend also, that is my answer.'
With a shout of delight Alain urged Bronn forward,
'I have thought of something that is quite absurd,
Gwen, if you marry Sir Rhydian, you will be My Lady.'
This caused much laughter along the way to Brefi.
After a few days journey the town came into sight
Soon they reached Aldan's small house. No light
Was lit, no animals to be seen, the doorway closed
And barred. Gwen ran to the old byres, she called
For her mother, but no voice answered. The stable
Lay empty, the hayrick bare, in the straw a sable
Coloured cat slept unworried by their presence.
'Where is our Mam, I am fearful, for this absence
Is not her way.' Gwen suddenly stood still, head
Bent in the breeze, listening intently, then she led
The way to the river bank gazing into the water.
After a long silence, she spoke. 'I can sense her,
But not see, she is well.' Tears of relief flowed
Down her face. 'I have need of her, she showed

Greatest love for my brother, but we grew closer
After he died. She must know that her daughter
Has found true happiness and share in her joy.'
Alain stood by her and together, maid and boy,
They sent their thoughts for the river to carry
To Aldan along the water, there for her to see.

Another Companion

That night they slept in the stable on sweet hay,
The chill of the early autumn night held at bay
By Aldan's cover and the warmth of the hounds
As they jostled for a place. Soft, rustling, sounds
Broke the quiet, mice running across the stone
Flags, watching for the barn owl as it flew home
To roost. As dawn broke a man silently entered
The barn, disturbing no one as he gently settled
Himself in a corner, waiting until their innocent
Dreams had run their course, much like a parent
Watching over their children. The rising sun cast
Its light though the open door, chasing the last
Of the nights shadows away, painting a golden
Halo on the sleepers. Rhydian, first to be woken,
Lazily stretched his cramped limbs, unfocused
Eyes resting on the stranger, unsure he puzzled
To make sense of the shape, suddenly he leapt
To his feet, grasping the hilt of his sword, kept
Close by. The figure spoke gently, 'Be at peace
I am no danger, an older, and wiser man, I cease
To look for combat, even when I'm sorely tried
I seek to find another way.' A bright eye belied
The age, yet the truth of his words was found
In the stillness and easy manner of the hound.
'I have word entrusted to me for the children
Of Aldan, the fair maid's beauty would soften
The hardest heart, so was her mother in years
Gone by. I loved her too well, even the tears
She shed for another did not lessen the power
She held over me.' As the sun threw longer
Shafts of light into the stable the others began
To stir. Gwen, giving a loud cry of delight ran

To their visitor, 'Yvain, do you bring me word
From my mother?' Halting, her voice faltered
Waiting for his reply. Gently he brushed a tear
From her cheek, then replied. 'Have no fear
She's been gone a sennight now, but where
I do not know, tho she set off in good cheer
With word that I was charged to keep guard
Here, to watch for you to return, my reward
To see your sweet face again, and to meet
The man with whom I must now compete
For your affection.' Laughingly, he kissed
Her hand, 'Good knight, I have oft wished
Gwen was mine, but not for a sweetheart,
As a daughter, 'tis Aldan that has my heart.
When my brother left to follow his Prince
I stayed to give her comfort, and ever since
Have been near, waiting for the sun to rise
On the day when it is me, not him she sees.
You are much blessed to have Gwen's love
She is like her mother's twin, and will give
Herself to but one man.' Rhydian laughed
And then replied 'But I am doubly favoured,
For I also have gained her son's friendship,
I fear I will never escape, they have a grip
On my life that I cannot break, nor ever
Desire to. I would consider it an honour
If you would travel with us on the final
Part of our journey, I will keep my rival
With me, surely 'tis much safer that way.'
In high humour they left later in the day.

Nearing Home

A happy party rode along the banks of the Teifi
Meeting the old road by the Clywedogau valley.
Once again Rhydian travelled the path of dreams
No ghosts troubled him as they crossed streams
And climbed the mountain tracks. Passing close
By the mines he told tales of soldiers and holes
In the ground, of treasures found, rescues made.
They camped on high, as the light began to fade.
Gathered around the firelight their stories grew,
Leading into the land of magic and myth, new
Music flowed from Rhydian's crwth, till sleep
Overcame them all. In the moment before deep
Slumber claimed him, a mantle of love covered
Yvain, removing the pain of years, he savoured
The warmth in his heart and slept until morn.
Their journey continued taking the well-worn
Way to Llanymddyfri. 'Rhydian, your hounds
Must be named, they are half-grown, it astounds
Me you have not yet done so.' 'I take the blame,
When small they were but the ci bach, no name
Was needed, later, they had an understanding,
Needing no telling of our minds, just knowing,
Yvain, yours shall be the honour, choose well.'
'You put a heavy charge on me, your noble
Hound dog has the aura of kings, like his sire
Before him, the bitch, is gentle, but with fire
Inside her. Alain loves her like a sweetheart,
So she will be Carys. There will be no upstart
Name for your little warrior, for he will bear
His father's name, he has proved he is an heir
Worthy to be called Cabal.' With the naming
Agreed they continued to the castle, rising

From a small hillock above the river plain,
Under whose walls many a battle for gain
Had been fought. As the end of his journey
Drew nigh, he reflected back to the carefree
Youth he had been just a few months past.
He mourned for that lost boy, who too fast
Had grown into manhood. He had put aside
The dreams of childhood, taken with pride
Another road, leading to discovery of true
Friendship and love, a gift given to but a few.
Yet would that be enough? He was unsure
Of his welcome home, for he returned a poor
Knight, no riches to share, no place at court,
And no tales to tell of great battles fought.
He looked at the old road he had travelled,
Lonely hills he had crossed in untrammelled
Days of freedom. Just for one moment he stood
Poised for flight, to leave the binds of manhood
Behind. Scarcely had the thought arisen when
It died away, his future was here, with Gwen,
They would face life's uncertainties, and build
A foundation together, happy and fulfilled.

The Fletcher

The river cut a valley between steep hillsides
Thickly lined with trees, where game hides
From view. The river meandered, dwindling
In size until just a mountain stream. Finding
Themselves in an open place they made camp
Lighting a fire to rest by. A grey mist, damp
In the night air, encircled them, like a blanket
Cold and sombre, while an unearthly quiet
Descended on the forest behind, no sounds
Reached them. Gwen shivered, the hounds
Drew near, pressing their warm bodies close
To her, giving her courage. Yvain's arrows
Lay beside him, spilling out of their quiver.
Gwen picked one up, stroking the feather
Fletching, 'I remember seeking for these
With my mother, but for her, only geese
Would do, they chased me, though frightened
I would never show it.' At this Yvain smiled,
'When we were children Aldan could cozen
The perfect feathers from the hardest man,
I could find the straightest Ash tree, knowing
Which branches to cut, then Bron, climbing
Higher than any other, brought down the best
To take home. Bron may have been the finest
Archer for many a mile, but 'twas me who made
The truest arrows. Many's the time we played
Tourneys, with Aldan bestowing the victor's
Prize, always to Bron, she was my brother's
Devoted slave and I was hers, I never ceased
To love her and I have no wish to be released.
I still live in the hope that one day she will see
Yvain, no more a little brother, and give to me

Just a portion of her heart. So I keep watch over
Her and hers and wait, for I am a patient lover.'
The morning broke with the sun chasing away
The final threads of the autumnal mist, a day
To savour, where the air was crisp and clean,
A gentle time before winter arrived and keen
Winds brought the driving rain, and snow filled
The mountain passes. 'I cannot ply my skilled
Hand to make arrows without the wood I need,
I would explore these forests. If you are agreed
Alain will come to help me, we will not delay
Your journey for long, lest you wish this day
To reach Castell Du, a hard ride but within
Your reach if you dally no further but begin
Now.' Rhydian laughed, 'I find I have a strange
Reluctance to return, I feel there is a change
In me that will not take kindly to a mother's
Rule once more. You go with your brother's
Son, you will enjoy each others company,
I recall hearing tales of an ancient yew tree
That grows deep in yon woodland's heart.
The morrow is soon enough for us to depart.'

Alain

The two young lovers rejoiced in their company,
Too few were the times they had alone, a free
Day, with none to care for, was a rare treat.
They told of their hopes and dreams, of sweet
Memories they held dear, of sadness and joy
They shared silence and soft song, as every boy
And girl who truly loved, have since time began.
Their peace was shattered suddenly, Yvain ran
Into their camp. 'Come quickly, I fear for Alain
He is hurt, I need your help, I tried, but in vain,
To stop him, hurry.' This said, he ran back into
The woods, not a backward glance as the two
Followed, until coming shortly to a small glade.
There, as if sleeping, lay Alain, under the shade
Of a giant chestnut tree, the gentle Carys beside
Him. Gwen halted, with a fear she could not hide,
'Is he dead?' she whispered. Rhydian knelt down
Feeling the still body, touching his face. A frown
Crossed his brow 'No, though he breathes but
Faintly, I can see no injury. Yvain, tell me, what
Happened?' ''Twas the castan, he said you loved
Them and tonight you would have hot roasted
Chestnuts by the open fire, I told him the tree
Was old and the branches not strong, but he
Would not listen. Up he climbed to the highest
One and leant across, then with the mightiest
Crack the branch broke, he fell to the ground
Like a stone, there he lay, with not a sound
To be heard, and scarcely a breath passing
His lips, although I have no understanding
Of these matters, I know he is in great need
Of skilful help.' His voice faltered, 'I plead

With you Rhydian, for in your knightly training
You must have gained knowledge in dealing
With such injuries – tell me he will not leave
Us.' 'I cannot give such assurance, believe
Me I would that I knew. I learnt from Brother
Thomas how to set a bone and how to cover
Wounds, but he has no wounds, no broken
Bones that I can feel, no, the hurt is hidden
Inside his head, he must rest undisturbed
Tonight. Gwen, fetch our blanket for a bed,
Yvain, make a shelter, cover it with bracken
Then pray that in the morn he will waken.'

Gwen's Mission

All night long Rhydian kept vigil, wishing
For the healing waters that were flowing
Over Emrys' cup in that cave so far away.
The long night ended as the breaking day
Lifted the dark shadows from the forest.
Gwen stirred, her sleepy gaze focused
On the slender form of Alain, she laid
Her hand gently onto his brow, afraid
To touch the pallid skin. Rhydian held
Her close, the rising fear that dwelled
In him kept hidden, 'I have the need
For help, with just my instinct to heed
I know not if I do right, we were told
As squires to make such wounded hold
On to speech, nor allow them to sleep,
For they might not wake again or keep
Their wits. Brother Thomas believed
Otherwise, that a body, rested, healed
Best. You must ride in haste and seek
My home, fetch my mother, I can speak
Well of her powers, for she is close kin
To the healers of Myddfai, wherein
Lies her skill. Cadair will safely carry
You, trust him and he will be your key
To enter the castle gate, for all know
He lets none ride him bar me. Follow
This pass between the hillside, be bold
As you reach Trecastell's stronghold,
Take a wide track, keeping well away
And travel fast here, brook no delay
Ere you are passed, then go eastward,
Along the river, the way homeward,

There standing by its banks, the castle.
As you approach the bridge, be careful
To keep out of the shadow and uncover
Your fair face, show you are no danger,
Then ask for the Lady Elaine, the guard
Will call her to you.' 'Rhydian, 'tis hard
To leave, cannot Yvain go in my place?'
'It must be you who goes, for this race
Cadair, the swiftest of horses is needed,
And I must stay here, for I have tended
Wounded men ere this. Now, be gone
See, Cyfaill is here too, you are not alone.'
He watched as horse and hound flew
With their precious burden, they knew
The trust placed in them, they would
Not fail to care for his lady. He could
But hope and pray for help to guide
Her until she was again by his side.

Waiting

It was with a heavy heart he watched
His beloved Gwen leave, he prayed
For her swift return and safe passage
To his home, with her quiet courage
Sustaining her along the lonely way.
He returned to Alain where Carys lay
On constant guard, Yvain spoke softly
'You must rest, the boy sleeps deeply
Yet, I will rouse you should he wake.'
Before the dream world could take
Him into its hold it seemed music
Surrounded him, so pure its magic
Weaved around his soul, a potent
Power, that came from the ancient
Days when man was liken to a child,
Simple in his belief, not yet defiled
By the greed of all men. He slept
Until shaken hard, startled he leapt
To his feet 'Come quickly, I need
Help, he awakes, and does not heed
Me, Rhydian, I know not what to do.'
The boy cried out, his unseeing blue
Eyes stared in fear, sweat drenched
His hair and body, his arms flailed
In the air. Holding his hand tightly
Rhydian stripped off the covers, he
Bathed him with cool spring water,
'We must keep him from harm, rather
He was still than this, his mind needs
To remain untroubled. See, he heeds
My voice, Yvain, fetch me my crwth
I will play to him, its music will sooth.'

As the sweet notes flowed from the bow
Yvain looked on with sadness, 'Long ago
My grandsire gave that to Emrys, he bade
Him search hard for the man who played
With his soul, it was his greatest sorrow
That none of us was such a man, now
I can hear the beauty of Joseph's thorn
Weave its magic again, from the dawn
Through the night it will bring peace
And comfort, giving its own release.
I have a boon to ask, that you will sing
To us, it will ease my heart, and bring
Closer to earth God's healing power.'
As he sang, silence fell like a cover
Over the land as every living being
Ceased for one minute, listening
To a timeless prayer. As the sound
Died, there followed a profound
Moment, as if mankind was reborn
All evil vanquished in a new morn.

Castell Du

Cadair's fast pace took them swiftly through the green
Meadows that lined the river, heading toward unseen
Tracks following the ancient path through the narrow
   pass.
Their speed slackened as the way grew bare, the grass
Gave way to stones as they climbed higher, the chill
Wind from the east blew straight over the high hill.
Gwen shivered with the cold, drawing her cloak
Tightly around her slim body, as the sun broke
Through the grey mist warming her with its pale
Rays. The path descended to the river, to a trail
That led to the long abandoned castell, standing
Guard over the river plain, having seen fighting
Over long years, now for many it was providing
Shelter. Approaching warily, Rhydian's warning
In mind, Gwen bending low over Cadair's side
Urged him on, needing no such spur he replied,
Travelling so fast that none could keep pace,
Beyond the range of arrows, a headlong chase
Beneath the hills and woods, through marsh
Lands, until they reached the river, the harsh
Track had given way to lush meadows where
Cattle grazed. The land was familiar, the air
Seemed to echo to words, 'Hurry, God speed
My child' all along the water's edges the reed
Swayed and sang, water, thrown by galloping
Hooves, surrounded her like a spray of loving
Hands, holding her safe as tiredness overcame
Her, desperately she clung to the thick mane.
Sensing her strength waning, Cadair quickened,
Eager to bring his charge safely home, a bend
In the river brought the castle walls into view.

A great Bailey surrounded the castell, a new
Tower arose from the motte, a stone gateway
Sat between earthen banks. A wood bridge lay
Over the deep ditch, ready to be withdrawn
If any attack threatened, guards ready to warn
Of strangers approaching. As they drew near
A cry went out – 'They come!' – pathway clear
They entered. The great horse, sides heaving
Shuddered to a halt, where a woman, waiting
Eagerly, took his rider into her arms. 'Be still
We are ready, come and tell all, but wait until
You are within, the Lady Elaine is also eager
To hear.' Squires appeared to care for Cadair
And Cyfaill. Gwen, looking into Aldan's face,
Too tired to question, sank into her embrace.

The Lady Elaine

Elaine came towards her across the bailey yard
Until she reached Aldan's side. She looked hard
At the young girl who stood there tall and proud
Bearing herself with a quiet dignity, and found
Herself warming to her son's lady. 'Your mother
Has been waiting eagerly for news of your brother
She knew yester eve all was not well, but could not
See him, nor you, until you passed Trescastell fort,
Came into her sight, then I too saw and followed
You along the river to Castell Du. When all is told
I leave with my sergeant at arms, we can travel fast
He will be my protection on the way.' Gwen cast
A stricken look at her mother's face as Aldan cried
Out in protest, 'He is my son, it is my place beside
Him.' Elaine held her gently, 'My sister, trust me,
I have much knowledge in these matters, I can see
To his hidden wounds, for there the danger lies.
Time is of the essence, there must be no delays.
You must prepare a litter to convey him home
Then follow after, this will travel slower, some
Time tomorrow before you arrive. Gwen will
Show you and your company the way, be still
This is how it must be.' Aldan replied, with grief
In her voice, ''Tis but a short time for my belief
In you to yet be strong enough for me to give
My son into your care, I beg of you, let him live
For I lost one son, I cannot bear to lose another.'
Gwen watched in awe as Aldan, her strong mother,
Let another go in her place, conceding to a skill
Greater than her own. 'My Gwen, we must fulfil
Our part of the bargain, fetch warm soft bedding,
We will get ready to follow as soon as able, bring

211

My bags too, for I also have many herbs and lotions,
Given me by Emrys, old magic is in these potions.'
Cyfaill, tired, but sure, led Elaine's party, retraced
The way she had but shortly come, as Gwen placed
Her hand on her mother's arm, 'Alain is strong
He will be causing mischief, I warrant, ere long.'

Rhydian Sleeps

Alain sleeping uneasily, stirred whenever
The music ceased. The tired crwth player
Drifting into slumber only to be recalled
As fretful movements returned, calmed
Only by the playing and the sweet sound
Of a voice, softly singing, so profound
That they brought with them a healing
Peace as the hours slipped by, seeming
To have no end. Into his half hearing ear
Came a hound's baying close by, with fear
He listened, this fear turned to great joy
As Cyfaill burst into the glade, and the boy
Within him cried as he saw the well loved
Figure of Elaine following. He embraced
Her, his words tumbling out one by one
As he led her to Alain. 'Hush, my son
You have done well, how did you know
To keep him quiet? I have seen a blow
Such as this fell a grown man, wrongly
Cared for the brain will not mend, the
Mind is a strange and unknown power.'
Rhydian replied, 'I just did what Brother
Thomas would have me do, the body heals
Itself he said, we just help it, until it feels
Right to leave. To stop his restless fever
I played to him, and sang, as I remember
You did to me when I was a child, it seemed
To soothe him, I am very tired for if I stopped
He became fretful again.' With a growing regard
For her son, Elaine laid hands on her new ward.
'I can tell the blood of Nelferch runs strongly
In your body, you have done well, now I see

You are in need of rest, sleep well, I will care
For Alain now. You must be ready for the fair
Gwen to return. You could not have been wiser
In your choice, she is all I wish for in a daughter.'

Rhydian Awakes

In his dreams a young maiden placed a kiss
On his lips, leaning over him with tenderness
And great love, he smiled and reached out
To hold her. The vision faded and he sought
To find her again, he ran over the hills, calling
Her name, waiting for the chill wind to bring
An answer. His name came back, soft at first,
Then louder, he sought for the caller, a thirst
Driving him onward. Then he heard a joyous
Laugh, 'Rhyd, wake up lest we think Morpheus
Himself sleeps in our midst.' Still befuddled
By sleep, he stared up at the image, puzzled,
'Gwen, is it really you? Surely it cannot be,
It has been too little a time,' wonderingly
He reached out to touch her. She grasped
His hand and held it to her face, 'I asked
How long you had slept, it seems both
Day and night have gone, by my troth
You are a sluggard, I arrived ere dawn
Broke, we travelled all night, this morn
I find you here, senseless to my touch
And snoring like a twrch, I have much
To tell you, you must listen in silence
To my story, for that is your penance
For the tardiness with which you greet
Me.' Though the words were hard, a sweet
Smile belied them. 'Alain, how does he?'
'Fear not, his greatest danger now will be
Keeping two broody hens from smothering
Him, each sure they are the one knowing
How best to restore him to full strength.
Their rivalry in healing goes to any length,

See here is one coming now.' She pointed,
Smiling as Elaine, drawing near, seated
Herself close by. 'I must return home now,
Alain is over the crisis, and Aldan knows how
To care for him. You two must also leave
With me, Yvain agrees to stay, and I believe
Aldan now sees in him a man to love and trust,
He is rare, a man who can love without lust.'
She was silent for a moment, then with sudden
Determination stood up, 'Do as you are bidden,
I will not allow the mother for my grandchildren
To stay one more night in these woods, my men
Are ready to return, we will be back by nightfall
Then we must prepare for the feastday. I recall
My wedding, many people from miles around
Came, it took much planning, and I'll be bound
This will be the same, you have but one day left
Of freedom and pleasuring, then you will be bereft
Of her company, for such closeness is not seemly
Nor right, before you're joined in holy matrimony.'

Part Eight
The
Wedding

No Gainful Employ for Rhydian

In the castle stables Rhydian sat on the straw
Beside Cadair, Cyfaill's head, and Cabal's paw
Resting on his lap. He sighed and aimlessly
Kicked the dust away, mice ran harmlessly
Along the walls, seeking odd grains that fell
From the trough. 'My friends, can I re-tell
You the story of when I first saw her smile?
I have written a song to her, for all the while
She is in my heart, shall I sing it to you again?
Enough, I will go to seek friends, you remain
Quietly here, for the castle is full to bursting
And yet more come, as if the son of a king
Were marrying, not an insignificant knight
From the princes of old, whose bride might
Be beautiful, but of birth lowly and unknown.'
In the village he found the crowds had grown
With all manner of visitors, minstrels, jugglers
Camping outside the bailey walls, mummers
Too, with garlands strewn across their tents
Bringing colour and gaiety to all, with sights
And sounds from far away, giving short respite
From the drudgery and daily toil, every minute
Saved, to be retold on dark nights. He walked
Unknown among the crowd, as people talked
And laughed, they greeted old friends, made
New. Ahead lay the church, children played
Outside, and within all was noise and bustle.
No priest at prayer, but candles and crystal
Lighting the dark corners, signs of festivities
To come on the next day, bright nosegays
And Green foliage covered the altar table
Making all ready. Yet on the eve of his special

219

Day Rhydian was unnoticed, played no part,
He returned to the castle with a sore heart.
There, drawn by the smell of new baked bread
He entered the kitchen, where shadows danced
On the white washed walls, thrown by the glow
From a mighty fire, here batches of fresh dough
Warmed, until ready for baking. Taking a pie
From the table, quickly, lest the watchful eye
Of the cook noted its absence, Rhydian looked
Around the crowded room, no hand dawdled.
Then he spied a small boy standing by the fire
He, alone of all there, seemed sad. His attire
Was black with soot, tears streaked his face
He swayed with tiredness, he tried to place
Himself beside the fire, but stumbling, fell
To his knees in the hot embers. With a yell
Of warning Rhydian ran to him, and lifting
Him up, brushed the ash from his clothing.
'What do you here, so close to the heat?
Your hands are sore with blisters, your feet
Too, firstly tell me your name.' The boy replied,
'I am Vonn, one of the spit-boys, I have worked
All day without a break, with still more tonight
To roast, and tomorrow the Ox.' His sorry plight
Caused Rhydian much pain, that a child so young
Could suffer for him. He removed his jerkin, flung
It down, placing the boy on it to rest. 'I will turn
The spit tonight, you sleep. I have much to learn
Before tomorrow dawns.' Vonn watched in awe
As the stranger took the lowliest of roles, a poor
Serf's place. His soft voice began to sing, bringing
A restful sleep to the child, others, all unknowing
Of whom the singer was, listened. Feeling a peace
Enter their spirits, they worked without cease.
Later, with all ready for the morrow, gathering

In friendship, sharing tales and songs, lingering
By the hearth. This was the scene that greeted
The Lady Elaine, who seeking her son, entered
Unheard. The harsh words that rose inside her
Died before they reached her lips, for no anger
Could stay where love flowed. 'Come my son,
You have tarried long, your work here is done
Now you must return to the Castle, your Bride
Awaits you, so too the Priest.' 'Pray, do not chide
Me, for today I have learnt much and received
More, also found hardship that I had not believed
Lay so near to me.' Vonn held safe in his embrace,
He followed the Lady Elaine to his destined place.

The Wedding Day Dawns

The sun had not yet risen when Rhydian awoke
On his wedding morn, a mist hung like a cloak
Over the sleeping valley, the distant hills rising
Above, with the moon's silver light touching
The peaks, as if covered in snow. He watched
As the sun's rays grew stronger, then turned
The silver a rosy hue, dawn breaking on a day
That comes but rarely, keeping winter at bay.
Leaving his room he walked across to the silent
Stableyard. With his Cadair there was no urgent
Need for action, no hustle. All too soon the castle
Stirred and Rhydian returned to his more formal
Duties, the order of service, greeting the guests,
Yet still no sign of his Gwen, despite his requests
To have word with her, she remained closeted
With the womenfolk, kept apart, Alain laughed
At his discomfiture, and vowed never to marry.
Noon approached, Rhydian donned his finery
With pride and rode through the village, cheers
Rose from waiting crowds as he passed by, tears
Blurred his vision at the outpouring of goodwill
That flowed over him. Turning to look at the hill
Where the castle stood he saw the bridal party
Led by the priest, wending its way, flowers gaily
Strewn before Bronn, carrying her sweet burden.
As they reached the church, Alain took Rhydian
By the arm, leading him to his place, past people
Known and unknown, voices creating a babble
Of sound. Time stood still as he waited, longing
For old friends, who were far away, belonging
To another time. He felt, rather than heard
His Bride approach, slowly he turned his head

THE WEDDING

In trepidation, afeared they would hide away
The simple essence of his beloved's beauty.
He held his breath in awe, her gown glowing
With the reflected light of candles, flowing
Like a cloud. Hanging round her neck he saw
A leather thong holding a stone ring, she wore
No other adornment. Her long dark hair worn
Loose as maidenhood decreed, flowers borne
In her hands, but in her hair none, just a circlet
Of gold, ancient, crafted in love, their eyes met
And they were alone. Her hand was placed
In Rhydian's and the wedding commenced.

The Wedding Over

With the final blessings of the marriage
Given, their vows taken and the pledge
Made, the first nuptial kiss lingering
On their lips, ready for the wedding
Feast, a black feather slowly floated
From high above. As it softly landed
At their feet the candlelight flickered
And time stood still. Figures appeared
Reaching out to Rhydian and his lady,
A warm breeze caressed them, gently,
Lovingly. The gates of Annwn opened.
For a moment the two worlds shared
A common realm, then the doorway
Closed, and time returned to their day.
Holding the feather, Rhydian searched
The clear skies outside in vain. Saddened
He knew than Menw would no longer fly
That this had been their final goodbye.
They walked among the village people
Speaking to all on the way, feeling humble
In the presence of so many. They danced
On the green, sang with the minstrels, fled
The mummers japes until finally entering
The hall, where their guests were waiting.

The Wedding Night

Rhydian and his new bride lay quietly
On the great bed, now alone strangely
Shy, not touching each other, keeping
Their thoughts to themselves, feeling
Unlike the two friends who had shared
Dangers and laughter, who had pledged
Themselves to one another a short while
Ago. Rhydian turned with a rueful smile,
'My lady, I am not at ease in this gloomy
Room, I feel as if many eyes watch me
I long to show you my love, but here
I cannot.' Gwen smiled, her eyes clear
And bright, she took his hand 'Come,
I know where we shall go, I too, long
To leave this bed, we will sleep easy
Elsewhere, and I know the place to be.'
Together, like naughty children bent
On mischief, they dressed and crept
Through the Castell, past drink-filled
Sleeping guards, to the stable yard,
There led a startled Cadair out through
The gatehouse. They rode down to
The river-bank, the cares of the day
Forgotten as the moon lit their way
To the place where Rhydian had first met
Gwen, though just a reflection of her spirit
As she slept, so far away. 'When I saw
You then, I loved you, and as long as I draw
Breath will so do.' There, where it had begun,
United in body and spirit, they became as one.

Epilogue

The twin suns of Draconis cast double shadows from the space ship, throwing them long over the blue grass. Two young people stood on the hilltop, viewing their new homeland. They watched as the engines fired up, sending red hot jets of flame down onto the black stones of the landing site, unable to hear each other speak above the noise. Holding hands they watched as the ship took off, speeding into the sky, not to return again for many months. The youth reached into his pack, and opened a leather pouch, handling it very carefully he drew out a thin circlet of gold, with a stone of the deepest blue set in an ancient clasp, which he gently placed on the girl's long black hair. 'In my family the eldest son is given this ancient symbol of love, for him to keep until he finds his soul mate. I want you, Ganieda, to accept this as the outward symbol of my love.' With a soft smile the girl replied. 'I too have a gift for you, in my family the eldest daughter is given this ancient symbol of love, for her to keep until she finds her soul mate. I want you, Maczen, to accept this as the outward symbol of my love.' She took a stone ring from a leather thong worn around her neck and placed it on his finger. Then keeping each other close they walked through the strange landscape to begin a new chapter in a never-ending story of their love.